D1633727

Bethlehem
love
story

Bethlehem love story

The romance of Ruth

KENDALL DOWN

AUTUMN

HOUSE

About the author

Kendall Down has an education in theology, experience as a pastor and is a published writer. He lives with his wife and family in North Wales. A Welsh speaker Pastor Down is well known as a preacher in the chapels of a variety of denominations.

Other titles by the author

Claudette, an historical novel.

Daniel, an exposition of the historical background and prophecies of the Bible book.

Copyright © 1995 by Kendall Down

First published in 1995

ISBN 1-873796-51-X

Published by
Autumn House
Alma Park, Grantham, Lincolnshire
NG31 9SL, England

CONTENTS

Bethlehem

'Just over the next hill, dear. We should be able to see Bethlehem from there.'

Ruth smiled at her mother-in-law, but said nothing. The road up through the forest from Jericho had been long and arduous, despite their pre-dawn start. The water in their old and leaky water-skin had given out as they came within sight of the Mount of Olives. The last two miles to Jebus had exhausted the two of them as Ruth all but carried the older woman up the final slope to where they could drink from the cool water of an irrigation channel in the Kidron Valley.

They rested side by side beneath a fig tree, gazing up at the massive walls of the Canaanite stronghold, until the sun began to lose some of its fierce midday heat. Ruth stood up, helped her mother-in-law to her feet and the two women trudged up the slope away from Jebus and towards Bethlehem, a mere two hours' walk away for a healthy woman, three if she was tired at the end of a long journey.

As they neared the top of the hill the forest of acacia and cedar gave way to a grove of olive trees. The dusty track led from shade into the bright light of open fields. Naomi halted and pointed to a tiny cluster of huts surrounded by a rough stockade of stones and mud walls. 'Bethlehem — the House of Bread.'

If Ruth was disappointed at the size of the village she didn't say so. Naomi had not tried to gild her words, but the exile's longing for home had undoubtedly had its influence on her description of her home town.

'Where is your house, mother?' Ruth asked.

Naomi peered across the hills, squinting her eyes into the evening sun. 'It's hard to tell from this distance,' she admitted. 'Mahlon's father owned that field over there, just to the right of that vineyard and he owned a couple of olive trees on that slope beyond the village.'

'I suppose he sold all that before you came to Moab to escape the famine?'

Naomi looked up sharply at the discouraged tone. Ruth was usually so cheerful. 'Oh, yes, but we'll get it back. You'll see.'

'Us?' Ruth laughed bitterly. 'How? We've barely enough money to buy our food for the next month. How are we going to buy land and trees?'

'We don't need to.' Naomi said, starting to walk towards Bethlehem again. 'It's only another three or four years to the Jubilee.'

'What's the Jubilee, mother?'

'Don't you know about the Jubilee?' Naomi stopped and looked searchingly into Ruth's face. 'No, I don't suppose you do. I'm sorry. I should have explained it to you before we left Moab. You see, no one in Israel can ever really sell their land, because all the land belongs to Yahweh. What you do is, you sell the right to use the land. Then, every fifty years, in the year of Jubilee, all the land that has been sold goes back to its original owners and everybody starts off equal again.'

Ruth slowly put down her bundle and rubbed her aching shoulder. 'Is this true?'

'Of course.' Naomi assured her. 'That's the Law Yahweh gave us when we first came out of Egypt.'

Ruth's face suddenly burst into a beaming smile. 'Oh, mother! What a wonderful God your . . . *our* . . . Yahweh is! What a wonderful Law. We're going to be rich!'

She threw her arms around the older woman and swung her round in an impromptu dance of happiness.

'Well, not rich,' Naomi corrected her when Ruth finally let go, 'but we should have enough to live on — if we work hard and if Yahweh sends the rain.'

'We'll work hard.' Ruth promised, as she picked up her bundle.

'Did Yahweh give you any other laws like that?' she asked as they set off down the path again.

'There are lots,' Naomi assured her. 'Our God is a loving God who really cares for the poor people. For example, if we are in need we can go to someone richer and borrow money and the lender is forbidden to take anything we need — like a cloak or a millstone — as security. If our only security is a cloak, then the lender must give it back every night so that the poor person has something warm to sleep in. Also, of course, Yahweh forbids usury, so we don't have the terrible debt problem that you have in Moab.'

Ruth shook her head slowly. 'I'm so glad I decided to worship Yahweh. He's much nicer than Chemosh. All Chemosh ever wants is more sacrifices. He doesn't care for poor people.'

'There's another thing,' Naomi continued. 'If you have sold your land, a rich relative can redeem it for you at any time.'

'Redeem it?'

'Yes. Buy it back. He goes to the person who has bought the land and pays him back the purchase price — or less if he's had the land for a while and reaped several crops from it — and then the land is yours again.'

'But what if the man who bought the land doesn't want to sell it back?'

'But that's just it. He can't refuse! He has to let the

land be redeemed — so long as it is the original seller or a member of his family who is offering to redeem it.'

'Have we got any rich relatives in Bethlehem?' Ruth asked.

Naomi thought for a moment.

'No one in our family has ever been *really* rich — and anyway, I don't even know if any of them are still alive. Perhaps they all died in the famine. Anyway, although the buyer must allow the land to be redeemed, there's no law to say that a relative has to redeem the land. I doubt that any of my relatives would be wealthy enough to redeem Elimelech's land just so that they could hand it over to us.'

As the shadows lengthened into evening the two women climbed the last hill to the entrance of the village and stopped by the well that stood just outside the gate. The group of women standing gossiping fell silent as they approached and stared at them suspiciously.

'Some water, neighbours, for the love of Yahweh.' Naomi called.

A young woman tittered and several of the others scowled.

'Who are you calling "neighbours"?' an elderly woman shouted and bent down to pick up a stone.

Naomi gaped at them in disbelief and Ruth pushed forward to stand protectively in front of her mother-in-law. Even as she did so another woman, middle-aged and plump but still handsome, came out of the village gate and walked to the well. She joined the group of women, stared at Ruth and Naomi a moment and then, face wreathed in smiles, waddled towards them.

'Is it really you, Naomi? I can't believe it! We all thought you were dead.'

'Naomi!' exclaimed several of the women.

'Is that Naomi?'

'I would never have recognized you!'

The women crowded round Naomi and Ruth, their hostility forgotten, smiling, chattering, welcoming. A girl ran into the village, shouting the news as she went and soon more people came pouring out of the gateway.

'Where's Mahlon's father?'

'Where are your sons?'

Naomi had been dreading that question. She held up her hands.

'Don't call me Naomi any more. Call me "Bitterness" instead, for Yahweh has dealt very bitterly with me. I went out full and Yahweh has brought me back again empty.'

There was a moment of shocked silence and then one of the older women drew her head-cloth down over her face and began the shrill lamentation for the dead. Others joined her and soon Ruth and Naomi were surrounded by a circle of women, weeping in sympathy for their sorrow. A tall, well-dressed man on the outskirts of the crowd, his beard slightly flecked with grey, put both hands to the neck of his garment and ripped it slightly, then bent down and scooped up a pinch of dust which he sprinkled on his head.

'Who's that?' Naomi asked, suspending her keening to nod towards the middle-aged man and question the woman next to her.

The woman looked in the direction she had indicated. 'That's Boaz. Don't you remember him? — Salmon's son, you know, the chap who married that prostitute from Jericho.'

She broke off suddenly and put her hand across her mouth. 'Sorry! I forgot. He's related to you, isn't he?'

Naomi nodded. 'Yes, quite closely in fact. My, hasn't he changed! Last time I saw him he was barely out of his teens. How's his father?'

The other woman shook her head. 'Dead, I'm afraid. That famine was just too much for him. And

Rahab died not long afterwards — of a broken heart, some say.'

'So who has Boaz married?'

The other woman grinned and slapped Naomi playfully. 'You'll never guess! He's not married at all; and he's the most desirable bachelor for miles around. He's got his father's land and then one of his mother's brothers died without children so he got his land as well. He's rich, I tell you.'

Naomi nodded thoughtfully and then the two women began to wail and lament again, beating their breasts in the traditional ritual of mourning.

The laws mentioned in this chapter:
Jubilee — Leviticus 25:23-28.
Surety — Exodus 22:25-27.

A place to live

Naomi and Ruth spent that night in the crowded court-yard of a relative's house. In the morning, after the men had gone out to the fields, and the children to shepherd the flocks, Naomi and most of the women in the village sat in the sun outside the house and talked, their fingers busy with weaving or cleaning the grain for the mid-day meal. Ruth, her face half veiled in the presence of so many strangers, sat and listened.

When the visitors had gone to prepare the meal for their returning men, Naomi took Ruth aside.

'It is as I feared, dear. None of my relatives is rich enough to redeem our land, and of Mahlon's father's relatives there's only Boaz and Machir. Machir is cer-tainly wealthy enough but he's the most notorious skinflint in the tribe of Judah. You'd never get him to part with any of his money, not to two women who will probably never be able to repay it.'

'Well, what about Boaz?'

Naomi shook her head. 'I'll certainly make sure he knows of our situation but I'd be too ashamed to ask him straight out. He's much younger than I — closer to your age, really. When I last knew him he was barely out of his teens; now he's a grown man. If his father were still alive it would be a different thing but . . .' She shrugged her shoulders and let her voice trail away.

When Naomi's relative came back at midday he brought word that there was a tumbledown, one-roomed mud hut outside the village that they could use. Normally it was occupied by men or boys guarding the crops against the depredations of wild animals such as the herds of deer that still roamed the hills. Of late it had become too decrepit even for that. If Naomi and Ruth wanted to try and fix it up, they could use it for as long as they needed.

Later, while Ruth and Naomi were standing outside the hut discussing the best way of repairing the holes in the roof and the crumbling walls, a young girl came and told them that the headman's wife was willing to pay half a measure of wheat per day if either Naomi or Ruth would come and help her around the house. Ruth left with the girl at once, leaving Naomi to sweep out the hut and arrange their pitifully few possessions.

When Ruth returned just after sunset she found a crowd of men swarming all over the hut and Naomi standing by in tears. Ruth hurried up to her.

'What's wrong, mother? What are they doing?'

Naomi turned to her and flung her arms about the younger woman. 'Isn't Yahweh good! Ruth, these are our relatives and neighbours. They've come to repair the house. Look, the walls are fixed already and they say they will do the roof tomorrow.'

That evening they ate at another relative's house and as they were leaving the man pressed a sack containing several measures of wheat into Ruth's arms.

'Take it,' he said, when Naomi tried to demur. 'It's my tithe.'

Naomi thanked him and they both left. As soon as they were out of earshot Ruth asked, 'What's tithe?'

'A tithe is a tenth of your increase.' Naomi answered.

Ruth nodded. 'But why was he giving it to us?'

Naomi smiled, her teeth flashing through the darkness. 'That's another one of Yahweh's Laws. Every year we have to put aside a tenth of our increase for the priests.'

'A whole tenth!' Ruth sounded indignant. 'Even the priests of Chemosh don't demand that much!'

'Ah, but you forget. You have a king as well. In Israel Yahweh is our king and the priests are His ministers. They are our judges; they teach us how to read and write so that we can learn God's Laws; they protect us from oppression and they are ready to help out wherever there is need. You wait. Our Levite will come round soon enough to see if he can help us.'

'So why did that man give us his tithe? We're not priests.'

'No. Everyone also has to pay another tithe — or rather, they have to set it aside to spend when they go up to Shiloh to worship Yahweh every year. They can spend it on whatever they like; new clothes, better cattle, equipment for the farm, a slave to help around the house, anything at all. Only they must spend it at Shiloh.'

'What good is that?' Ruth sounded puzzled.

'I'll tell you, my dear. You know old Machir, the stingy one I was telling you about? If he had his way, his wife and children would go around in rags, even during the festivals at Shiloh, but because he has to spend a full tenth of his increase there, at least his wife gets a new dress and some jewellery every year and the children get some toys as well.'

'My!' Ruth turned to her mother-in-law, her eyes shining. 'Isn't Yahweh a wonderful God! Why, I know someone back in Moab — you remember Ishbaal? His brother is exactly like Machir, and his wife does have to go around at the festivals dressed in rags. She feels so ashamed and embarrassed.'

'Then there's the third tithe,' Naomi continued, 'which we only pay every third year. That has to be given to anyone who is poor — widows like me, orphans, or strangers like you. If there's any left over, it goes to the Levite who usually knows someone in need.'

'So that's why he gave us the grain?'

'That's right. Yahweh will care for us, you'll see. I suppose that if He wanted to He could cause the birds of the air to bring us food, but He tells us to share what we have — probably to teach us not to be selfish.'

Ruth suddenly stopped. 'Do we have to pay tithe?'

'Oh, yes.' Naomi assured her. 'No one is exempt. Of course, a tenth of what you are carrying there won't come to much but we'll give it to the priest in the morning. We'll put some aside for when we go up to Shiloh and in two year's time I'm sure we will be able to find someone worse off than ourselves to whom we can give the third tenth.'

In the morning Ruth accompanied her mother-in-law to the priest's house, a small building of mud bricks roofed with straw thatch, just like the houses around it. Both women drew their headscarves across their faces before Naomi called for the priest.

'Are you there, my lord?'

There was a short delay and then the curtain across the door was pulled aside and a tall, slim man in a once-white robe stood before them. He raised his hand in blessing.

'Yahweh be with you, my daughters.'

'My lord,' Naomi continued, 'I — we have returned from Moab to the land of my fathers and I bring to you our tithe.'

She turned to Ruth and lifted down the cloth-wrapped bundle she was carrying on her head, then squatted down and undid the knot that gathered it up and divided it into two.

'May Yahweh bless you.'

The priest turned and went back into his house, returning a moment later with a large clay jar. He lifted the lid and watched as Naomi poured the two cupfuls of grain into the jar. 'And what is that for?'

He pointed to the small pile of flour that remained in the second half of the cloth.

'Yahweh has been good to us, my lord. He has brought us back safely to the land of my fathers, so this is a thank offering.' Naomi hesitated, and then continued slightly faster: 'I'm sorry, my lord, but I don't have any frankincense.'

The priest smiled. 'Don't worry, my daughter. Let's call it a peace offering, then you don't need the incense.'

'But can you offer flour as a peace offering?'

The priest frowned slightly. 'Strictly speaking, no. It ought to be made into loaves of bread.'

He stroked his beard and thought for a moment. 'I'll tell you what; I've just remembered that I was going to make a peace offering of my own — a vow or something — and I really ought to do it today. Now that peace offering of yours wouldn't go very far, but if you join with me we should be able to invite quite a few people. Would you do that for me?'

Naomi stared up at him and slowly nodded. The priest extended his hand.

'Thank you, my daughter. It so happens that I'm rather busy today and it would be difficult for me to visit many people. Would you do me the favour of going round and inviting people to the feast? I'll leave the guest list to your discretion. Now, let me bless you.'

Naomi hastily gathered up the cloth, carefully rewrapping the flour, and both women stood, heads bowed reverently, while the priest pronounced the blessing over them.

'May Yahweh bless you and keep you; may Yahweh make His face shine upon you and be gracious to you; may Yahweh lift up His countenance upon you and give you peace.'

Naomi and Ruth walked slowly away. As soon as

they were out of earshot Ruth turned to her mother-in-law.

'What's a peace offering, mother?'

'It's one of the types of offering that Yahweh commanded us to offer, my daughter. You bring the food or the animal and offer it to Yahweh. The priest takes a small part of it, to show that Yahweh has accepted the offering and then we feast and make merry with what is left.'

'With that bit of flour?' Ruth stifled a giggle. 'You'd better not invite too many people.'

'Ah, but don't forget that the priest is going to include us in with his offering.'

'Yes, but still don't invite too many people. That way there will be more for everyone.'

'That's true, but you see, we have to eat all the food today. Any that is left over in the morning has to be burned.'

Ruth halted, her mouth open in astonishment. 'Burned! But that's a waste!'

'I don't know,' Naomi shook her head. 'Food, particularly meat, doesn't last, especially in summer. I think, though, that Yahweh had another idea in mind. If you could keep on eating the food for as long as you liked you wouldn't invite others to join in, but because you have to eat it up in one day — two days if it is an offering you have vowed to Yahweh — you invite everyone you can think of and then, if there's still food left over, you give it to the poor. I expect we'll be very glad to be invited to share in peace offerings before we are much older.'

Ruth smiled and hugged her mother-in-law. 'Of course! That's Yahweh helping out the poor again. I wonder why He is so interested in people like us? I thought gods were only interested in people who could give them big offerings and rich gifts.'

Naomi took Ruth's hand and started to walk again. 'The difference is that Yahweh isn't like the other gods. He doesn't need offerings and gifts, because He made everything — the whole wide world. He even made Moab.'

'Do you think Yahweh made Chemosh?' Ruth asked.

Naomi thought for a moment. 'I think He must have, because Yahweh made everything. But,' she held up her hand and wagged her finger for emphasis, 'I'm very sure that Yahweh didn't make Chemosh the way he is. I think Chemosh must have gone wrong somehow.'

They walked in silence for a moment and then Ruth remembered something else that had puzzled her. 'Why didn't we prostrate ourselves in front of the priest, mother?'

Naomi started to laugh.

'What's so funny?' Ruth demanded.

'Nothing, nothing,' Naomi chuckled. 'Just the thought of prostrating ourselves in front of Ithamar. I can just imagine the look on his face!' She laughed heartily again. 'No, my daughter, we do not prostrate ourselves before anyone except Yahweh. Ithamar is only a man — a special man, perhaps, but only a man like any other man. We show him respect, but we would never prostrate ourselves before him.'

———

The laws mentioned in this chapter:

    Tithe — Numbers 18:21-29; Deuteronomy 14:22-29; 26:12.

    Thank offerings — Leviticus 2:1-3.

    Peace offerings — Leviticus 7:11-21.

    Priestly blessing — Numbers 6:22-27.

The peace offering

When they reached their hut Naomi sat down outside the door, her back to the wall, and began to compile the guest list, scratching names onto a potsherd she had picked up outside the village gate.

'There,' she said, holding out the potsherd to Ruth. 'That should be enough. That's all the people who have helped us, plus all the priest's family that I can think of. You go to the ones who have helped us and I'll go round the priest's family. Just tell them that Naomi is making a peace offering out of thankfulness and that they are invited to come to the High Place.'

Ruth hurried off into the village. The first person on the list was the relative who had been so kind to them. She didn't dare speak to the man of the house; anyway, he was probably out in the fields, working. Instead she delivered her message to the man's wife, a short, plump woman with a squint in one eye who was busy sorting through a tray of peas when she called.

'Mahlon's mother says that she is making a peace offering this evening and can you and your family come to the High Place,' Ruth told her.

'Is she now!' The other woman stopped cleaning the peas. 'Tell her that we'd be delighted to come. What is it? A thank offering or something?'

Ruth nodded. 'Yes, that's right.'

'Good. Listen, you don't happen to know, is anyone else bringing peas?'

'What do you mean?'

'You know, peas.' The woman gestured at the tray in her lap. 'I'll bring these peas I was going to cook them for tonight anyway, but I don't want to upset someone else if they were planning to bring peas.'

'But Naomi invited you,' Ruth protested. 'You don't have to bring anything.'

'Yes, but . . . .' The other woman smiled up at Ruth. 'You see, I can't really come without inviting my neighbour next door and I shouldn't think she's on your list. I can't just turn up with someone Naomi isn't expecting, so I'll bring along my peas and that will make up for it. Don't worry, dear, it's what we all do.'

The next woman on Ruth's list promised to bring some loaves of freshly baked bread, because she couldn't think of coming without her best friend. The third woman said that she had a nephew staying and she would have to bring him and his friends, so she would make up for it by contributing some raisins and a huge bundle of greens, and so it went on. Everyone insisted on giving something towards the peace offering meal and everyone knew someone else who simply could not be left out.

'I think the whole village is going to be there!' Ruth told her mother-in-law when they were both back at the hut.

'Oh, I expect so,' Naomi said, nodding her head placidly. 'I'd hate to think that anyone was left out.'

'Then why did we just invite a few?' Ruth wanted to know. 'Why not just invite the whole village and be done with it?'

'Ah, but we've honoured our friends and relatives by inviting them. They've invited the others. Now, come and help me turn this flour into bread.'

The High Place turned out to be a bare patch of rock on the summit of one of the hills overlooking Bethlehem. As evening drew on Ruth and Naomi climbed up the path to the High Place. Ruth had a bundle of firewood balanced on her head and a small pot with glowing coals in it, while her mother-in-law carried the bread, wrapped up in a cloth, the water-skin and a huge cooking pot borrowed from a neighbour. Half way up the slope Ruth paused and looked back, the bundle of wood swivelling slowly.

'Look, mother! Everyone's following us.'

Naomi glanced back. 'Of course. They wouldn't go there before us. This is *our* offering.'

As soon as they reached the High Place Naomi rolled three large stones together and set the pot down on them, then poured some of the water into the pot.

'Build the fire under here, my daughter.'

Ruth lowered the bundle of firewood and quickly broke up the sticks into manageable lengths, stacking them neatly beneath the pot. When the fire was ready she carefully placed one of the coals on the wood and bent over to blow it into flame.

The first to arrive was the priest, leading a fine, fat ram, its huge tail almost dragging in the dust.

'Here we are, then, Naomi,' he called. 'What do you think of that?' He pointed to the ram.

'Wonderful, my lord. A fine beast. What is your peace offering for?'

The priest shrugged and laughed. 'I don't know. I can't remember. Maybe it's just because you are back.'

Soon the High Place was crowded with men, women and children. One by one the women came over to Naomi and presented her with their gifts, a dish of cooked peas, some greens and spices for the pot, and endless loaves of bread that piled up beside the pot in a shiny brown heap. When everyone was there the priest, with a couple of other men, dragged the protesting ram over to the large, flat stone in the centre of the High Place and pushed it over onto its back.

'Friends,' he called, 'this is Naomi's peace offering

and I welcome you to the feast. Naomi, come and dedicate the sacrifice.'

Naomi stumbled forward, with Ruth by her side, conscious of every eye watching them.

'But this is your sacrifice, my lord,' Naomi protested in a whisper.

The priest smiled and shrugged again. 'Perhaps, but I think you should dedicate it.'

Naomi turned and faced the crowd. 'My friends, I thank you all. I intended to give a small thank offering to Yahweh — all that I could afford — but your love and your generosity have made this a real . . . '

Suddenly she burst into tears and hid her face in her head-cloth. Ruth put her arms around the older woman's shoulders and heard her whisper 'Thank you. Thank you all, and may Yahweh bless you.'

The priest stepped forward again and stood by the head of the ram. 'And may Yahweh bless you, Naomi. We are all very glad to see you back with us, so let us give thanks to Yahweh with the sacrifice of this ram.'

He stooped down and there was a flash of metal followed by a startled bleat from the ram that was abruptly cut off. The animal struggled briefly and then lay still while the red blood gushed out of its throat and flowed down to the ground.

When the ram was finally dead the men, watched with horrid fascination by all the boys in the crowd, proceeded to butcher it, carefully removing the skin and slicing down the belly to expose the entrails. The priest, meanwhile, took some of Ruth's firewood and lit a fire on the flat stone in the centre of the High Place. When the wood was blazing the priest placed the skinned fat tail, the kidneys and all the fat around the entrails onto the fire and watched while it smoked and burned.

'What's he doing, mother?' Ruth asked.

'Burning the fat and the kidneys,' Naomi answered, busy stirring into the pot the meat which the men were bringing her.

'But why?' Ruth protested. 'That's the best part.'

'I don't know,' Naomi replied. 'That's the part that Yahweh claims for Himself. Mind you,' she added reflectively, 'I sometimes wonder if even that isn't for our benefit. Have you noticed how few fat people there are in Israel? I mean *really* fat, like Abibaal the merchant back in Moab.'

Both women smiled, remembering the man who was so fat that he could hardly walk and had to have two slaves to support him wherever he went.

'I'm sure being that fat can't be good for you.'

As the smoke of the sacrifice drifted over the High Place and the twenty or thirty children chased each other in and out among the adults, the women clustered around Ruth and Naomi and helped with the preparation of the food. Young men flirted with the girls while the older men sat around the altar and discussed the crops and the news of Canaanite raids in the north.

An hour later the meal was ready. Ithamar, the priest, stepped forward and gave thanks to Yahweh for the food and then everyone crowded forward and received their portion, neatly placed on broad leaves stitched together with slivers of wood. To Ruth's amazement there was plenty for all, for the village headman and one or two of the richer elders had given generously. Even Machir the skinflint had been persuaded or shamed into providing a huge platter of parched barley and a tray of sweetmeats.

It was late at night before the feast broke up, with every scrap of food gone, and Ruth and Naomi found their way back to their hut, the good wishes of their friends and neighbours ringing in their ears. As they made ready for bed Ruth remembered something she wanted to ask her mother-in-law.

'Mother, why did Ithamar ask you to dedicate his sacrifice?'

'Because he didn't want to shame me,' Naomi declared, her hand poised over the wick of the oil lamp. 'He wanted everyone to think that I had provided the ram instead of barely enough flour for one small loaf of bread. He's just like his father.'

'How kind of him! I can't imagine any of the priests of Chemosh behaving like that. Oh, mother, is everyone who worships Yahweh good like that?'

The laws mentioned in this chapter:
Burning fat — Leviticus 3:6-11, 17.

Making ends meet

After the sacrifice at the High Place things seemed to change. A whole week went by before Ruth and Naomi were invited to another meal, and although the men came back the evening after the sacrifice to repair the roof, once that was done only the children came past, herding the sheep and goats out to their pasture beyond the village fields. Ruth went to work for the headman's wife every morning, washing and mending clothes, sweeping the house, cleaning the grain and preparing the vegetables for the evening meal.

As the shadows lengthened, she returned to the hut outside the village — where Naomi waited for her. Ruth lifted down her headscarf and emptied out the handful of vegetables and the small measure of grain that the headman's wife had given her to pay for her work. 'It's not much, mother.'

Naomi eyed the small pile critically. 'No, but it's not unfair. A day's work and a day's wages.'

Ruth laid her hands across her stomach and pressed in. 'Maybe, but I never feel as if I have enough to eat. The last time I was full — really full — was at your sacrifice.'

Naomi looked up at the younger woman, her face clouded. 'I know, dear. I feel the same way. It will be different when our garden starts producing, I promise. At the moment only the weeds seem to be prospering.'

'I'm sorry, mother. You've been doing the really hard work, digging the soil, carrying the water and pulling the weeds. How's your back?'

Naomi pressed her hands into the small of her back

and grimaced. 'I'll live!'

'Do you want me to rub it for you?'

'Well, when you've rested.' Naomi shrugged her shoulders. 'I'm not getting any younger, and that's a fact.'

Twenty minutes later, while the vegetables boiled briskly in the clay pot over the fire, Naomi lay down on her stomach and Ruth began to work on her back, kneading and pulling the tired muscles while Naomi passed on all the village gossip she had learned at the well. When the older woman was relaxed Ruth stood up and stepped lightly onto her back, treading up and down her spine while Naomi grunted with satisfaction.

'Now you stay there, mother. Don't move, while I make the bread.'

Ruth emptied the grain onto a flat, black stone and began to grind it into flour, rubbing back and forth with a lump of hard diorite that came all the way from Egypt, if the merchant was to be believed. The harsh grating sound, as the two stones rubbed together, settled down into a rhythmic push-pull that was soon matched by Naomi's deep breathing. Ruth glanced over at her mother-in-law and smiled, glad to see the older woman asleep.

At last the grain was all ground to coarse flour and Ruth dusted it off the quern into a flat clay pan, then added some water to make a soft dough. When the flour and water were thoroughly mixed she pinched off a small ball of dough and began to slap it rapidly back and forth between her hands, flattening it until she had a large, thin disk of dough. With her foot she nudged a hot stone out of the fire and then slapped the disk down over it so that the moisture in the dough sizzled and hissed as the unleavened bread cooked. She left it for no more than half a minute and then peeled it off the rock, flipped it over and baked the other side. When that was done she pushed the stone back into the fire while she flattened out another lump of dough.

When the simple meal was ready Ruth leaned over and rubbed Naomi's back some more until she was awake and able to sit up. The two women talked as they ate, the slow, easy phrases of companionship where each understands the other and is content in her company. As the meal was ending Naomi glanced over at Ruth's work-stained garment.

'You're going to need a new dress one of these days.'

Ruth shrugged. 'I guess this will last a while yet.'

'But you need a new one,' Naomi insisted.

'What I need, mother dear, is a rich husband,' Ruth joked. 'He can buy me a new dress — and buy our food so that you don't have to work in the garden any more.'

When Naomi made no response Ruth looked up, her face colouring in the silence. 'Oh, come, mother! You haven't found a rich husband for me, have you?'

Naomi shook her head and sighed. 'No, I'm afraid not.'

'Afraid?' Ruth laughed. 'I'm too old to think of marrying again, mother. Eighteen or nineteen? No one would even look at me. Anyway, I'm a childless widow. People probably think I've got the evil eye or something, otherwise why should my husband die and all this misfortune happen to us?'

'Rubbish!' Naomi snorted. 'You're in the prime of life. You're a hard worker, you cook well, you can carry a good load. Any man would be lucky to get you. You're even quite pretty — and just because Yahweh didn't give you any children by Mahlon doesn't mean you can't have any. It isn't always the woman's fault, you know.'

'Mother!' Ruth exclaimed, her face glowing with embarrassment.

'Well, it isn't,' Naomi insisted. 'I've known more than one case where a woman who was divorced for childlessness by one man had children — sons, even — by another man, while his next wife was also childless.'

Ruth said nothing, hoping that her mother-in-law would let the subject drop, but Naomi, her back resting comfortably against the wall, was in talkative mood.

'That's not to say that Yahweh doesn't hold some women back from bearing children. Take the case of Nahshon and Milcah, which happened before we went to Moab. They had been married for fifteen years without a single child; Milcah was never even pregnant. Then one day Nahshon came home to find a strange man in the house — a Midianite trader in embroidered work, if only he'd stopped to find out — and became jealous of his wife. Foolish, really, because there were servants just out in the courtyard, but that's the way some men are. Anyway, after brooding on it for several weeks, and poor Milcah in tears because of his constant accusations, nothing would satisfy him but he must drag the poor girl all the way up to Shiloh and go through the Trial of Jealousy.'

'What's that?'

'Well, the man and his wife go up to the tabernacle at Shiloh with two pounds of barley flour as an offering and the priest puts holy water and some dust from the floor of the tabernacle in a pot and makes the woman drink it. She has to let down her hair and swear that she has not been unfaithful to her husband, then the priest writes out a curse on the woman and washes the ink off the paper and into the pot and the woman has to drink that as well.'

Ruth shuddered. 'What is the curse?'

Naomi looked very serious. 'If she has been unfaithful to her husband, then according to the curse her belly will swell and her — you know, down there — will rot.'

Ruth shuddered again and clutched her arms about her body. 'But what if she's innocent?'

'Why then Yahweh opens her womb and she has a child.'

'What happened to Milcah?'

Naomi smiled happily. 'She had three sons, one after another, and two daughters.'

Naomi leaned forward and prodded Ruth with her forefinger. 'And do you know what? Nahshon claimed afterward that he never really doubted his wife's honour. He claimed that he just wanted an excuse to make her drink the bitter water so that Yahweh would grant her children.'

'He was trying to trick Yahweh!' Ruth exclaimed.

'I know — and you can't trick Yahweh,' Naomi smiled gently. 'But do you know? I think Yahweh saw just how desperate he was and took pity on him — or maybe it's just that Yahweh does have a sense of humour.'

'Has anyone ever been found guilty by the Trial of Jealousy?' Ruth asked.

Naomi shook her head. 'Very seldom. Most women, if they are guilty, either confess before they drink the bitter water and are stoned or they run away. I only know of one woman who was guilty and actually drank the bitter water and that was a woman called Tirzah who lived up in Ephraim and was married to a mean old man twice her age. The women who know her say that she drank the water as bold as brass but afterwards her monthly course came early and she nearly went mad with fear.'

'Did she die?'

'No, but she ran away to Sidon and the last I heard

she was living as a harlot among the Gentiles. I think that the real reason for the Trial of Jealousy is to deal with those husbands who are insanely jealous. You know what some men are like. You remember Eglon, back in Moab, how he made his poor wife's life miserable with constant, unfounded accusations? Well, in Israel all the wife has to do is insist on going up to Shiloh and drinking a drop of water — and it costs her husband two pounds of flour and the expense of the journey. Makes him think twice before accusing her again!'

'You said that those who confess are stoned to death. That's horrible.'

'Not all of them. Sometimes a woman's husband loves her so much that he will forgive her. But yes, just occasionally you hear of a woman being stoned to death.'

'But why did Yahweh command that? If someone has to be killed, wouldn't it be kinder to kill them with a sword or something?'

'Perhaps.' Naomi looked thoughtful. 'But then, you see, there would be the danger of a blood-feud. Not over an adulterous woman, but if there was a murder or something, then the avenger or whoever was chosen to execute the murderer would be in great danger from his relatives. With stoning, however, everyone has to take part, everyone has to throw a stone, and who is to say which stone actually killed the criminal?'

'I see.' Ruth stretched and yawned and suddenly smiled. 'Yahweh certainly gave you good laws. Blood-feuds are a real curse in Moab — and everywhere else. My own cousin was killed because his uncle had killed a man whose brother had killed my cousin's uncle's grandfather's nephew. I think it went even further back than that, but no one can remember. Now, of course, my family are looking out for a chance to kill someone from the other family and so it will go on, probably forever.'

The laws mentioned in this chapter:
>   Trial of Jealousy — Numbers 5:11-30.
>   Stoning — Joshua 7:25.

Sabbath rest

'Ooh, I'll be glad when sunset comes.'

'So will I! Yahweh be with you, my daughter.'

Naomi stood in the doorway and watched as Ruth hurried down the path towards the village. The sun had not yet risen but there was a lot to do before the Sabbath began, both in the headman's house and in their own. When Ruth was safely inside the wall around the village Naomi turned back into the house and began the first of the tasks that would fill her day.

As soon as the sun was up Naomi walked quickly down to the village well, one pot balanced on her head, the other resting on her hip. A group of women was there already but there was little of the usual bantering and gossip. The women exchanged greetings and one or two talked in low voices, but all hurried to fill their jars and pots and return home to the work that awaited them.

Naomi made many trips to the well, giving the garden extra water, for the morrow was the Sabbath and there would be no work done during its sacred hours. It was nearly noon when she finished that task and then she picked up her small bronze axe and headed for the forest. On the way she met several other women heading in the same direction to gather firewood.

Once again there was a quiet urgency to all their actions. The group walked faster than usual and when they arrived at the forest they split up with a minimum of conversation, each going to her own favourite spot — a fallen tree or one blasted by lightning — where she hacked and chopped until she had gathered a large bundle of sticks. As soon as she had enough each woman set off for the village, so that there was only one other, a young girl, waiting for Naomi when she staggered out under a huge bundle of slender branches.

'Can you manage all that, Aunty?'

'Of course,' Naomi answered proudly. 'I may be poor but I'm not weak.'

'Good. Let's go.'

'Were you waiting for me? That was kind of you.'

'Mother told me to. She said that it's not nice to have to walk back alone.'

There was a break in the conversation as they both saved their breath for the steep rise that confronted them. Once they were over the top the girl was the first to speak.

'Don't you just hate Fridays!'

'Why? What's wrong with them?'

'Oh, you know, all this work and rush just so that you can sit around for a whole day and be bored.'

'Sit around?' Naomi sounded puzzled. 'Why do you do that?'

'Well, what else is there to do?'

'Why, lots! Yahweh gave us the Sabbath to help us realize that there is more to life than just eating and working. It's a time when we can use our minds instead of our hands and feed our spirits instead of our bodies.'

'How do you do that, Aunty?'

Naomi smiled to herself. Her companion sounded curious.

'Well, for example: can you read or write yet?'

The girl stopped and looked at Naomi, the big bundle of firewood on her head swinging round as she turned. 'No.'

'Well, why don't you go along to the priest and ask him to teach you. His father taught me and I'm sure he'd be only too glad to have another pupil.'

'But only boys learn to read and write.'

'Well, I can read and write, so it's not just boys. Anyway, the reason why we learn to read is so that we can read Yahweh's holy Law — and girls need to know about God's Law just as much as boys.'

The girl turned away and started walking again but Naomi could see that she was intrigued. 'What else can we do on the Sabbath?' she asked.

'Let me see.' Naomi thought for a minute. 'We can go out and explore the land that Yahweh has given us. Haven't you ever wondered what is on the other side of the forest? Did you know that if you climb up on to that hill over there you can see the sea? That's where Sodom used to be, the city which Yahweh destroyed because the people were wicked.'

'I've never been that far.' The girl sounded impressed.

'That sea is very strange, you know,' Naomi continued. 'You can't drink from it because the water is terribly salty — I know, I've tried it! Some people say that you can't sink in it either, but I don't know about that.'

'When did you try it, Aunty?'

'When I went to Moab. Now, what else can you do on the Sabbath? What about hunting for birds' nests?'

'My mother says you shouldn't do anything like that on the Sabbath,' the girl objected. 'That's hunting for food.'

'I don't mean to collect eggs or anything like that,' Naomi replied. 'I mean, to sit down and watch the mother bird caring for her chicks. Have you ever sat and watched how often a mother bird feeds her young and how their funny little necks stretch up for their food?'

The girl shook her head. 'No, Aunty. I've always had to hurry home.'

'That's right. But on the Sabbath you don't have to hurry home. You can take the time to see how Yahweh cares even for the birds and gives them the wisdom they need.'

'Is there anything else we can do on the Sabbath?'

'Lots! Ask your mother to prepare some special food and you and your whole family can go out into the woods or up on to a hill and eat it there. Shall I tell you a secret?'

'Yes, please, Aunty.'

'When I was a girl about your age, I found a lovely spot down by that hill over there — that one with the big tree growing on it. There's a valley on the right of it — can you see it? — and down there in the summer, when everywhere else is dry and brown, some water stays in a pool and all sorts of flowers grow beside it. I used to call it my secret garden and go there nearly every Sabbath in the summer.'

Naomi stopped and a dreamy look came over her face. 'I remember once when I was sitting in the shadow of a large rock I saw a mother deer and her fawn came down to the pool to drink. They must have been no more than about ten cubits away.'

'How wonderful!' the girl breathed.

'And then there's things you can do for others.' Naomi started to walk again. 'I know that you help to look after your baby brother every day, but on the Sabbath you could take all your brothers and sisters for a long walk and let your mother have a really good rest. Or you could go and visit Granny Deborah. She only has her grown-up son and I know that older people love to talk to children. Get her to tell you about her father who fought with a giant, one of the Anakim.'

'A giant! Did he really?'

'You ask Granny Deborah. Another thing you could do is go out and gather flowers. There's Milcah the cripple, who sits in her house all day every day. Think how she would love to have fresh flowers to smell and enjoy. Maybe there are people who are sick who would also enjoy a breath of the outdoors.'

Naomi recounted this conversation to Ruth when she came home about mid-afternoon. Ruth nodded her head.

'Oh, yes, mother. There's plenty to do on the Sabbath, but do you know what I most enjoy about God's day?'

'What?'

'The chance to sit back and do absolutely nothing.'

Naomi chuckled. 'I know just what you mean, daughter. How was work today?'

'Not too bad. We did all the washing and cleaning yesterday, so all that had to be done today was preparing the food for the Sabbath and drawing enough water to last two days.'

Ruth tossed back her head-cloth and squatted down in front of the stove. 'As you can see, the headman's wife gave me enough for us to have plenty of food for tomorrow. I'll have the vegetables on the stove in just a moment and then I'll start on the bread. Maybe we could take our food tomorrow and go to your secret garden, if you wouldn't mind walking that far?'

Naomi laughed. 'I'm sure I'd love that. It would be just like being a girl again.'

Sabbath dawned bright and sunny, like every day during the summer. Naomi rose and stood in the doorway of the hut, stretching and yawning while birds fluttered past, chirping songs of praise to Yahweh. Ruth joined her and the two women stood and looked out over the fields where the grain was slowly ripening in the hot sunshine.

'Isn't it nice not to have to hurry.' Ruth put her arm around her mother-in-law's waist. 'Sometimes I wonder how on earth we managed back in Moab with no

Sabbath. How did we keep going seven days a week, week after week?'

Naomi nodded. 'I know. The Sabbath is truly Yahweh's gift to us. Rich people who don't have to work hard during the week can't really appreciate it, but we can — and do!'

Ruth laid her head on Naomi's shoulder. 'Yahweh looking after the poor again.'

'Yes,' Naomi nodded. 'And I'll tell you something else that those fields have reminded me about. Sometime next week the harvest will begin and then you'll be able to go out gleaning.'

'Oh, no!'

Ruth straightened up and stared, wide-eyed, at her mother-in-law.

'Ah, but things are different in Israel,' Naomi said. 'Back in Moab the poor had to sneak out at night and try to snatch a few handfuls of grain or pick the kernels out of the cracks in the ground. If they were caught the land owner would seize the grain they had so painfully gathered and leave them with nothing.'

Ruth nodded. It was a familiar scene. The poor person — usually a woman — standing, head bowed, lips trembling, as the rich man or his agent ranted at them, the confiscated grain, a tiny bulge in a tattered head-cloth, dangling from his hand. Usually that was as far as it went, but sometimes the rich man would call up his servants to give the culprit a thrashing, and as often as not he would keep the poor person's head-cloth as well as the grain.

'Things are different here,' Naomi continued. 'Yahweh has commanded that no one is to reap in the corners of his field or along the edges. That is left for the poor to glean. Any stalks of wheat that fall from the reapers' hands are not to be gathered up. They are left for the poor. If the reapers forget a whole sheaf when they finish work and leave it in the field, they mustn't go back for it. It is left for the poor.'

'We still have to look for it in the dark,' Ruth objected.

'No you don't. Gleaners go out with the reapers and follow along behind them. Obviously you don't get in the way of the workers, you leave a little distance between you, but you have the right to be there, just as much as they do.'

'And doesn't the owner of the field object?'

'Of course not. It's your right to glean. No one can stop you.'

'Oh, mother!' Ruth grabbed Naomi's hands and danced around her. 'Isn't Yahweh wonderful! Come on, let's hurry and go and take an offering to Ithamar. I'm sure we can spare a little grain to say "Thank you" to Yahweh.'

The laws mentioned in this chapter:
    Sabbath — Exodus 20:8-11.
    Gleaning — Leviticus 19:9, 10.

Village gossip

After the morning prayers, when Ithamar led the village in worshipping Yahweh, Ruth and her mother-in-law returned home and bundled up the food they had prepared the day before.

'I'll carry this, you lead the way,' Ruth said, picking up the cloth-wrapped platter by the knots and swinging it by her side.

The distance was further than Ruth had realized — and more difficult than Naomi remembered — but the two women were happily ensconced by the little pool long before the heat of midday.

'I didn't think it would be this far,' Ruth remarked as she spread out her headscarf in the shade of a large rock.

'I didn't either,' Naomi admitted as she sank down gratefully to rest. 'I'm sure miles weren't so long when I was young!'

Both women laughed and Ruth sat down beside her mother-in-law and leaned back against the rock.

'Where did you see the deer?' Ruth asked.

'Over there,' Naomi pointed. 'The mother led the way straight down that slope and the fawn followed her, though it frisked about all over the place. They drank just by that big stone and then the mother led the way down the valley.'

'I wonder why this pool is here,' Ruth mused. 'The rest of the valley is so dry and bare in the heat.'

'I used to wonder that too, but when I grew up I concluded that the pool is man-made. Do you see how straight that further edge is and the way it is raised up above the valley? If you go there you will see that the bank is made of stones that look as if they were cut square, which isn't natural.'

'Who could have done that?' Ruth asked.

' I don't know. Maybe it was the Anakim, the giants who used to live here. Maybe they built it to make a pool of water. Perhaps originally this was a much bigger lake that filled the whole valley, only now it has nearly filled up with soil and stones washed down from the hills.'

'That's something that has always puzzled me.' Ruth plucked at the tall stems of grass in front of her. 'Yahweh is such a good, kind God, yet I've always heard that He commanded you to kill everyone in this land. Back in Moab I was brought up on stories of how Yahweh ordered you to kill all the Moabite men — even the small boys — and all the married women. When I was little my mother even used to threaten me that Yahweh would get me if I wasn't a good girl.'

'Did she really?' Naomi sounded horrified.

Ruth nodded. 'Oh, yes. And I was terrified. I thought Yahweh was a terrible God, much worse than our Chemosh.'

Naomi sat silent for a while and then slowly nodded her head. 'Yes, I suppose I can understand why you might think that. The thing is, that Yahweh didn't want to kill anyone. When He promised to give this land to our father Abraham He said that Abraham himself would not receive the land because the Amorites were not yet bad enough to be destroyed. In fact, our people suffered four hundred years of wandering and slavery in Egypt, simply because Yahweh wanted to give the people who lived here more time to repent.'

'But how would the Amorites know that they ought to repent? Did Yahweh send anyone — any prophets — to warn them?'

'Certainly He did,' Naomi nodded vigorously. 'Abraham himself was a prophet, and he and his children showed by their lives and example what Yahweh wanted. As if that wasn't enough, there were also prophets of Yahweh among the Amorites.'

'What?' Ruth turned to stare at her mother-in-law in surprise.

'You remember how we pay tithes to Ithamar? Who do you think Abraham paid his tithes to?'

'Who?'

'To Melchizedek, the good king of Jebus.'

'The king of Jebus! But no one in Jebus worships Yahweh!'

'Not now, and I don't know when people there stopped worshipping Yahweh, but once upon a time they must have, for Melchizedek was a priest to Yahweh. Then there was Balaam, the famous prophet of Yahweh, who lived up in Aram Naharaim. Did your mother ever tell you about how your king Balak asked him to curse Israel?'

Ruth nodded. 'The only time Balaam's curses failed to work.'

'So you see, Yahweh tried hard to get the people to turn back to Him. Only when every attempt failed did He allow us to return to this land.'

'But why kill people?' Ruth persisted. 'There are many nations who worship their own gods, but Yahweh hasn't told you to kill them.'

'Let me tell you a story,' Naomi replied. 'It happened a long time ago, when I was just a girl. My best friend was a girl called Miriam and she had an older brother called Ishbaal.'

'Ishbaal?' Ruth looked startled. 'But that's a Canaanite name.'

'I know. Miriam's father was a food merchant and he became very friendly with another trader in Jebus. I think he called his eldest son Ishbaal as a mark of their friendship. Anyway, when I was about 7 or 8 there was a terrible year; the crops failed almost as badly as during the famine when we came to Moab. There was a plague among the cattle that killed off most of the sheep and goats, and Miriam's mother died in childbirth.'

Naomi was silent for a moment, her face sad as she remembered the tragic events of that far-off year. 'Miriam's father was distraught over the death of his wife. He had suffered particularly badly from the plague — I don't think he had a single animal left — and of course with the crops all gone there was nothing for him to market. Then, to top it all, Ishbaal fell seriously ill. I used to go round every day and play with Miriam and I can remember her father coming out to tell us to be quiet, because we were disturbing Ishbaal.

'One day I went round as usual but her father sent me away. He said that Miriam couldn't play that day, so I went away thinking she had some work to do, but a little later I saw her and her father walking up the hill behind the village. I called out to her but she didn't answer: perhaps she didn't hear me. I never saw her again.'

'Why? What happened?'

'Her father took her to the old high place which we no longer use, where there was a big stone pillar to Asherah. He tied her to the pillar and then piled wood around her and set light to it.'

'He burned her alive?' Ruth was horrified.

'As a Moloch sacrifice to save the life of his son.'

'Did it?'

Naomi shook her head. 'No. His son died two days later. That's when he went to Ithamar's father and confessed what he had done.'

There was a pause and then Ruth asked, 'What happened to him?'

'He was stoned to death, of course. The point is, if he hadn't been so friendly with those Canaanites — or if they hadn't been around to lead him astray — Miriam would still be alive today. That's why Yahweh told us to exterminate all these evil nations, because otherwise they would corrupt us.'

'But why the children?' Ruth persisted.

Naomi shrugged. 'Children grow up like their parents; corrupt parents give birth to corrupt children. Sons might feel that they had to avenge their parents, daughters would get married and teach their children evil ways, or lead their husbands to worship other gods. There are many reasons.'

Ruth shuddered. 'I suppose you're right. But don't forget, there's also the other side to it. People who kill other people become hard and cruel. Did you ever meet a man called Mesha back in Moab?'

Naomi furrowed her brow. 'The famous warrior?'

'That's right.'

'No, but I heard a lot about him.'

Ruth shuddered again. 'He was cruel! People say that when he went out to war he would show off his strength by finding a child — boy or girl — and then he would grab its ankles in one hand, swing it up and smash its head against the ground or the side of a house. Then he would laugh and grab another child.'

'War does terrible things to men,' Naomi murmured.

'Yet Yahweh ordered your people to do that to the Canaanites,' Ruth protested.

'Yes, but that was our fault.'

'What do you mean?'

'When Yahweh first promised to give us the land, He said that we wouldn't have to fight at all. He was going to send wasps and hornets ahead of us to drive the Canaanites out. At least it would stop our men becoming cruel and hard.'

'So why didn't He?'

'Because we didn't trust Him. God left the Canaanites in the land to test us, because they are so much stronger and more experienced in warfare than we are. The only way we can conquer them is with Yahweh's help and if we don't trust in Yahweh we are defeated.'

'Meanwhile the poor old Canaanites have to just sit tight, waiting to be exterminated.'

'No.' Naomi shook her head. 'Yahweh still hopes that they will change their ways.'

'Even though He has condemned them to death?'

'Did I ever tell you about Aunt Rahab?'

'Your aunt? But that's the name of a heathen goddess,' Ruth objected.

'Aunt Rahab was not an Israelite.' Naomi smiled. 'In fact, she lived in Jericho, the first city we captured when we came to Canaan. After your king Balak tried to defeat us by magic, we moved down from the hills of Moab and camped at Abel Shittim. The Jordan was in flood and we couldn't cross at first, so Joshua, our leader, thought that while we were waiting he would send spies to Jericho to get some information on the city.'

'How did they get across the river?' Ruth wanted to know.

'There were ferries and things. Anyway, when they arrived in Jericho they went to stay with Aunt Rahab, who was a prostitute.'

Ruth gasped and covered her mouth with her hand. 'But mother! That wasn't very nice.'

Naomi smiled knowingly. 'Aunt Rahab always insisted that it was all very innocent and that they only came to her because every inn was full with people forced out of their homes and farms by the floods and, of course, refugees fleeing from us, but I must admit I have often wondered.' Her eyes twinkled at Ruth. 'We know what men are like!'

The two women giggled and then Naomi continued the story.

'Anyway, even though the two men were disguised as traders, it didn't take long for Aunt Rahab to guess who they were. Their accent was different, they didn't swear by the gods as other traders did, and they didn't recognize the names of merchants in Moab whom Aunt Rahab had met in the course of her business. Finally, when Aunt Rahab served them a meal they didn't make an offering to the teraphim in the alcove near the window.'

'So what did she do?'

'She didn't do anything, not at first. The men went out to look round the town and while they were out a neighbour came bursting in with the news that her two visitors were Israelite spies; a Moabite woman who had visited the Israelite camp and escaped the subsequent war happened to see them and recognized them. Aunt Rahab nearly died, because she had already made up her mind to serve Yahweh and she was afraid that if the men were caught she wouldn't get a chance.'

'A chance to do what?'

'Well, she had heard that Yahweh wanted to kill everyone in Canaan and her first plan had been to cross the Jordan and pretend to be from Moab or Ammon, but with the floods she couldn't get across. She was afraid that once we crossed the Jordan we wouldn't accept her.'

'So what did she do?'

'To her relief the two spies came hurrying back just before dark, their faces pale and anxious. She instantly took them up onto the roof where she was drying flax — her usual business was slack as all the men in town were too worried about the Israelites to think about other things.'

The two women giggled some more.

'Aunt Rahab piled the flax on top of them and when messengers came from the king to arrest the two men she pretended that they had sneaked out of the city just before the gates closed. She even said that she had overheard them planning to get back to Abel Shittim that night. One of the messengers hurried off to organize a pursuit while the other stayed to search the house — Aunt Rahab said it wasn't too difficult to distract him when he reached the roof.'

'Oh?' Ruth raised her eyebrows.

'I once asked her what she meant and she said I was too young to understand, so I waited until I was married and then asked her again, but all she said was that if I didn't know by then, I would never know.' Naomi started to laugh. 'Aunt Rahab was always mysterious like that.'

The two women clutched each other and laughed until their sides ached. Finally Naomi sat up and wiped her eyes.

'Aunt Rahab's house was built on the wall, so during the night she tied a rope to a heavy box and the men climbed down to safety, but not before she had made them promise that when the Israelites captured Jericho they would spare her and her family.'

'Why did she decide to join you?' Ruth asked.

'She remembered hearing about how Yahweh divided the Red Sea for us when we came out of Egypt and she knew how He had helped us to defeat King Sihon and King Og. The gods of Canaan had not answered any of her prayers, and she decided that she wanted to serve a God who could.'

'So when Yahweh made the walls of Jericho fall

down and everyone else was killed, your Aunt Rahab was spared!'

'That's right. Even though she was a Canaanite and a prostitute, Yahweh welcomed her. Her past was in the past; she started a new life when she joined Yahweh's people. Later on my Uncle Salmon married her and nobody thought any the worse of her. It was the same with the people of Gibeon.'

'Yes, tell me about them,' Ruth urged. 'Aren't they sort of temple slaves?'

'Well, this is what my father told me. Mind you, he was only fairly young when it all happened. Not long after Jericho was captured some men came into the Israelite camp dressed in the oldest clothes you have ever seen. Their donkeys looked worn out, their water-skins were patched and leaking and their supplies were all dry and hard — the bread even had mould growing on it.

'They asked to speak to Moses and seemed surprised to learn that he was dead. Joshua came to see them and they told some story about having come a long distance because they wanted to worship Yahweh. To prove how far they had come they claimed that their clothes were new when they set out and their bread freshly baked and rather stupidly Joshua believed them.'

'Why was that stupid?' Ruth asked.

'Oh, really!' Naomi glared at her in mock anger. 'If you set out on a long journey, which would you take: all the bread you might need on the way or a supply of money to buy fresh bread at each night's stopping place?'

'Of course!' Ruth exclaimed. 'And if your clothes wore out you would buy new ones, especially if you were some sort of ambassador.'

'That's right.' Naomi smiled. 'Anyway, Joshua and the other elders were completely taken in. They should have had a woman on their council. They made a solemn covenant with the men, swearing to them in Yahweh's name. Three days later they discovered that they had made a treaty with the Gibeonites, who lived just up the road and were one of the nations Yahweh had ordered them to destroy.'

'Why didn't Yahweh warn them and stop them making such a mistake?' Ruth wondered.

'In the first place, because Joshua and the elders didn't bother to ask; it all seemed so clear-cut and straightforward to them. Secondly, I think that Yahweh didn't want them to ask but if they had, I'm sure He would have told them to go ahead and make the covenant. Yahweh wants to save people, not destroy them.'

'So why are they slaves?'

'When a single person — like Aunt Rahab — joins us, they are on their own and surrounded by Hebrews. It's easy for them to forget about their old customs and habits and adopt Yahweh's ways. Here, however, was a whole nation, still living in their own cities, all helping each other to remember the old ways. Yahweh made them slaves to the tabernacle so that they would more easily learn about His Law and identify with it and with Yahweh. After all, even if you are only bringing water and firewood, it is still an honour to serve in the House of Yahweh.'

Ruth said nothing, so Naomi continued: 'Then there's another example: a little Moabite girl who was rather afraid of Yahweh but one day said that she would come to Canaan and serve Him. Do you remember? "Your people will be my people, and your God my God." '

Naomi quoted the words softly and Ruth raised her head slowly and looked at her.

'Daughter, when you said those words Yahweh heard you and immediately took you under His wings.

You became one of His people, just like any one of us. Why, who knows? Perhaps, if you marry again and have children, you might be the mother of the Messiah.'

'Me?' Ruth laughed and shook her head. 'I'll never marry again, mother. I'm too old. Nobody would want me.'

'Maybe.' Naomi looked serious again. 'But never forget: Yahweh wants you. He loves you. You are as precious in His sight as our father Abraham, for just as he left his home to come to Canaan, so you have left your home and entered into the covenant with Yahweh. You are His beloved daughter.'

————

The laws mentioned in this chapter:
    Extermination — Deuteronomy 20:16-18.
    Hornets — Exodus 23:27-33; Judges 2:20-23.

The runners

It was a still, hot day. Even the sparrows seemed to be panting in the heat. Ruth hacked irritably at the branch that dangled by a thin strip of bark from the tree above her and at last succeeded in severing it. The bough crashed to the ground beside her, snagging her skirt with its gnarled twigs. She carefully untangled her garment and then began the laborious task of reducing the branch to pieces of wood small enough to carry.

She scowled as the axe-head stuck fast in the wood and tugged cautiously at the handle, wriggling it back and forth until the axe came free again. The leather thongs that bound the bronze head to the handle were fraying again and she needed to keep a careful eye on them. Last time they broke the axe-head went flying off into the shrubbery and she had had to search for quite a while before she found it again.

The axe came free with a jerk and Ruth lowered it to the ground. She rested for a moment, leaning on the axe-handle and brushing a stray lock of hair out of her eyes. The day was too hot for hard work and her every movement was slow and measured. She fanned her face with a corner of her head-cloth and looked down towards the village and its white houses, surrounded by a sea of golden grain.

Idly she scanned along the path towards Jebus which ran out on the far side of the village and climbed the slope to the crest where it disappeared into the forest. As she watched, a tiny figure emerged from the trees and started down the track. Ruth stared in astonishment, for the man, little more than a dot at this distance, seemed to be running. She shook her head over his folly and then felt a sudden tightening of fear in her chest. Was he a messenger from somewhere, with news of a Canaanite raid or an advancing army?

She was both relieved and puzzled when the man carried on past the village, following the track that led to Hebron. Too curious to stay where she was, Ruth quickly collected her belongings, gathered up the wood she had cut and tied it into a bundle which she hoisted onto her head. Trying to appear calm and unhurried, she strode out of the forest towards the village, timing herself so that she would cross the stranger's path.

'Yahweh be with you.'

Ruth modestly drew the edge of her head-cloth across her face before returning the stranger's greeting. 'And also with you, my lord.'

'Is that a water bottle you are carrying?'

'Drink, my lord.' Ruth handed him the clay pot and watched as the stranger drank greedily, tipping his head back to devour every drop of the liquid. He was an older man with a neatly trimmed beard and the material of his loincloth was finely woven and probably expensive. She noted the foam that ringed his mouth and the sweat that darkened his garment.

'May Yahweh bless you.' The man held out the now empty water bottle and wiped his mouth with the back of his hand.

'And you also, my lord. It's a hot day for running.'

Ruth waited expectantly. News in exchange for a drink was a fair bargain, particularly on so hot a day. At least the man could explain where he had come from and why he was running.

'Is this the road to Hebron?'

'Yes, my lord.'

Without another word the man set off up the track, forcing his trembling legs into a stumbling run. Ruth clutched her water bottle and stared after him, frowning. Such abruptness was rare indeed, and unlooked for in a man who used Yahweh's name. As the stranger disappeared over the rise Ruth shrugged, slowly swung her load round and trudged on towards the village.

At the bottom of the low hill on which the village stood Ruth stopped in the shade of a straggly tree to rest before the ascent. She turned her head, swinging her load in a ponderous arc, to look along the path towards Hebron but the running man had disappeared. She turned back again, her eyes following the route the stranger had taken. As she glanced up to where the Jebus track left the forest she caught her breath. A second man had appeared, running down the path towards her. Ruth watched him in astonishment, far too curious to feel fear or to want to carry on up to the village.

'Yahweh be with you, my lord!'

'Eh? What?' The young man lurched to a stop beside Ruth, his chest heaving, the sweat streaming down his face. 'Water.'

The youth, no older than Ruth herself, raised his arm to wipe the sweat out of his eyes. Ruth's eyes widened at the naked dagger he held in his hand. 'Water, sister. For the love of Yahweh.'

'I'm sorry, my lord.' Ruth gestured with the empty water bottle. 'I gave every drop to the man who came running by not ten minutes ago. He . . . '

'Yahweh curse him!' The young man cut her short. 'Which way did he go?'

'He ran right past the village.' Ruth gestured along the path behind her. 'The path to Hebron.'

She almost shouted the last words as the young man, his face contorted with fury, set off up the track, staggering from side to side with weariness.

'Two of them!' Ruth exclaimed as she retold the story of her encounters to Naomi. 'I never knew that people who worshipped Yahweh could be so rude. They just ran away, without saying goodbye or anything.'

'And you say that the second one was carrying a knife?'

'More like a dagger,' Ruth mused. 'And he was only young, too.' She chuckled. 'It looked as if he was chasing the other one, but I guess that's just my imagination.'

'Oh, I don't think so,' Naomi assured her. 'I suspect that he was chasing the first man, and would kill him if he caught him.'

'Kill him?' Ruth exclaimed, her eyes wide with astonishment. 'But that's dreadful.'

Naomi shook her head.

'Maybe, but I suspect he has the right. Don't you know about Hebron?'

'I know the old stories about Caleb.' Ruth spoke defensively. 'It's one of the towns given to the priests, isn't it?'

'Yes, but it's more than that. It's one of the cities of refuge.'

'What's a city of refuge?' Ruth asked, squatting down beside her mother-in-law.

'Well, you know that if one man murders another, the relatives of the dead man — particularly his eldest son — have the right to kill the murderer? An eye for an eye, a tooth for a tooth and a life for a life.'

Ruth nodded. 'Of course. It's his duty.'

'But what if the man who did the killing didn't intend to kill his neighbour? Suppose it was an accident? Suppose they were out cutting wood and the head flew off one man's axe and struck the other man?'

'I suppose,' Ruth sounded doubtful. 'I suppose that in that case the killer wouldn't deserve to die. Mind you, very likely the avenger of blood wouldn't stop to ask questions.'

'That's right. That's why Yahweh commanded us to

set aside six cities of refuge, three on this side of Jordan, three on the other side. If one man kills another, the killer must run as fast as he can to the nearest city of refuge, where he will be safe from the avenger, but if the avenger catches him before he reaches the city of refuge, he can be killed without any guilt.'

'Mother!' Ruth was horrified. 'Do you mean that that first man was a murderer?'

'Probably.' Naomi nodded placidly. 'A killer, at any rate.'

'And the young man would be the dead man's son, trying to avenge his father.'

Naomi nodded again. 'I wonder if he'll get to Hebron before the avenger catches him? They were both equally tired?'

'Exhausted.' Ruth spoke crisply, then glanced down at the pot she was still holding. 'Ugh! To think that a murderer has drunk out of this!'

'We don't know that he is a murderer,' Naomi reproved her. 'Perhaps he killed by accident. I guess we'll find out at the trial.'

'What trial?'

'Oh, there'll be a trial, just as soon as the village elders reach Hebron. If he can satisfy everyone that the killing was accidental then the avenger has no claim on him.'

'What if he deliberately murdered someone?'

'A murderer has to pay with his life. That's only right.'

'Or his purse.' Ruth sounded bitter. 'The rich pay compensation, only the poor die.'

'Certainly not!' Naomi shook her head vigorously. 'For most things, yes. That's what the ''eye for an eye and tooth for a tooth'' business is all about. If I knock out one of your teeth you can knock out my tooth —

but only one, mind you — which is a powerful incentive for me to offer realistic compensation.'

Naomi chuckled, remembering an incident from her youth. 'There was a rich merchant from Egypt came through here when I was a girl. I forget why he couldn't go on to Jebus that night, but anyway he stayed in our village. He was a proud and arrogant man in fine linen with a big staff with a large ivory knob: the headman's house wasn't nearly good enough for him. You should have seen him looking down his nose at everyone and everything .'

'What happened?' Ruth prompted as Naomi paused, her eyes half closed.

'Everyone was scurrying around trying to serve the stranger and one of the headman's servants, a man called Elihu, tripped over a bag of merchandise and sent it flying. The Egyptian leaped to his feet and lashed out with his staff, hitting the man right in the mouth. I was there with all the other children, watching the show, and I can see the whole scene. Everyone except the Egyptian just froze and watched as Elihu slowly got to his feet, one hand clutched over his mouth and blood streaming down between his fingers. The merchant simply turned on his heel and went back to his chair as if nothing had happened.'

'Typical,' Ruth muttered.

'Of course Elihu quickly realized that one of his teeth had been broken off. He let out a yell and held up the broken piece and that's when things got serious. At first the Egyptian couldn't believe that anyone was bothered about a servant's tooth but when the chief spoke to him and he saw all the men of the village gathering around with angry looks and weapons in their hands he reached into his bag and pulled out a tiny piece of silver worth no more than a quarter of a shekel and held it out to the injured man.'

'Was that all he offered?' Ruth sounded indignant.

'At first,' Naomi grinned. 'Elihu started to shout and demanded his right to knock out one of the Egyptian's teeth. When this was translated to the merchant he was incredulous and yelled for his servants, but they were all unarmed and surrounded by village men with axes, so they couldn't help him. Someone handed Elihu a sharp flint, which he waved in the Egyptian's face.'

'That brought him down to earth a bit.' Ruth was clearly enjoying the fat merchant's discomfiture.

'More than a bit,' Naomi agreed. 'When the headman explained that under our Law the man had a right to one of the merchant's teeth and assured him that he would see to it that the job was done very carefully so that only one tooth was knocked out, the merchant turned a sort of green and started sweating. His next offer was two whole shekels.'

'That still wasn't much,' Ruth commented.

'No.' Naomi settled back against the wall more comfortably. 'Of course by now Elihu had worked himself up into a fine fury and nothing would satisfy him but a whole mouthful of the Egyptian's teeth but his father and his elder brother pushed themselves forward and carried on the bargaining. They demanded a hundred shekels and every time the Egyptian offered less they let the injured man do a bit more shouting and stone waving.'

'Did they get the hundred?'

'In the end they settled for forty. The headman acted as go-between, first taking them to one side and talking calmly to them and then speaking quietly to the Egyptian. Everyone was satisfied, particularly when the Egyptian added a small jar of perfume for Elihu's wife, to compensate her, he said, for having to kiss a man with a missing tooth. Not to be outdone she went out and spent the night cutting fodder which Elihu presented to the merchant in the morning, and he and his servants left amid smiles and blessings all round.'

'I suppose forty was a fair price for a tooth,' Ruth spoke slowly. 'What do you think a life is worth?'

'Nothing,' Naomi stated flatly.

'Nothing?'

'There is no blood price for a life. A life is too valuable for any money price to be set on it; even the life of a slave. Blood must be paid for with blood. A murderer is always put to death.'

'But what if he killed the other person accidentally?' Ruth asked.

'There can still be no blood price. He has to live inside the city of refuge until the high priest dies. If at any time while the high priest is still alive he steps outside the city limits and the avenger finds him, the avenger can kill him without guilt.'

'And after the high priest dies?'

'Then he can go back home.'

'But that's not fair!' Ruth burst out. 'What if the high priest dies the next day? Anyway, surely the dead man's family deserve some compensation?'

'I think the killer would be very foolish if he went back to his village too soon.' Naomi looked serious. 'The Law might allow it, but he would be taking his life in his hands unless he waited for tempers to cool. As far as compensation is concerned, although the Law doesn't set a figure — as I said, blood can only be paid for by blood — if the deed was truly an accident, the killer would feel terribly guilty for what he had done. He and his family would do their best to help the widow and orphans, so that when the high priest died he would have shown the extent of his sorrow and been forgiven.'

The following day a Levite from Hebron passed through Bethlehem on his way to Shiloh. The story of Ruth's double encounter was common knowledge in the village by then and the Levite was pressed for news.

'My brother was working in his fields on that side of town,' he told an interested audience. 'He heard shouting and when he looked around he saw the two men running down the road — well, running is perhaps too good a word. They were both nearly dead with the heat and stumbling along like a pair of drunkards. The killer was only just keeping in front of the avenger, who was slashing at him as he ran.

'My brother shouted at them, hoping to distract the avenger, but they were both so exhausted that they couldn't hear him. He ran over to them, but of course he couldn't do anything to interfere until they crossed the boundary of the village, so he just ran beside them, shouting constantly at the avenger, asking him questions, anything to try and distract him.

'Just as they came up to the boundary, which as you know is marked by a ditch and a stone, the avenger leaped at the killer and actually stuck his knife into the man's shoulder. The injured man fell to the ground and the avenger tripped over him and my brother knocked the knife out of his hand. By that time there was quite a crowd there so the killer was hustled away inside the city to have his wound bandaged and the avenger was taken before the judges. I've got to visit his village on my way north to ask the elders to come to Hebron for the trial, which should be in three day's time.'

'No,' he said, in answer to someone's question, 'the killer isn't badly hurt, a mere flesh wound. He'll be fine by the time of the trial.'

———

The laws mentioned in this chapter:

Cities of Refuge — Deuteronomy 19:1-13.

Eye for eye — Exodus 21:23-25.

Punishment for murder — Leviticus 24:17-23; Numbers 35:31-34.

The trial

'Can we go to the trial?' Ruth asked.

'Don't you have too much work to do?' Naomi teased and then, seeing Ruth's face, added, 'Of course we will. I imagine that everyone in the village, apart from Granny Deborah and Milcah the cripple, will be there. It must be years since there was a trial.'

'I suppose the harvest will start straight afterwards?'

'More than likely. The headman was out in the fields this morning after you went to work. He seemed satisfied with the way the barley was coming on.'

'And then can I go out gleaning? I wonder if the headman's wife will mind if I don't work for her during the harvest?'

'I'm sure she'll understand.' Naomi sounded confident. 'I'm too old to go out gleaning, so I'll go and help her a bit in your place.'

Early in the morning of the third day Ruth and Naomi set out for Hebron. When Ruth looked around in the grey light of dawn it seemed that everyone in the village was coming as well, but, as the light strengthened, she realized that none of the old folk was there and some of the young men were missing as well, left behind to guard the crops, she supposed.

The journey to Hebron was accomplished to the sound of singing, happy shouting and the excited yelling of the children. Along the way the people from other villages joined them and when they came in sight of the city they saw crowds flocking in from all directions, the white robes of the men gleaming through the clouds of dust their passage raised.

'Are these all Israelites?' Ruth asked Naomi.

'Of course, my daughter. A trial like this has nothing to do with gentiles.'

Everyone seemed to be heading for a wide area of open ground in front of the city. As they approached, Naomi tugged at Ruth's sleeve and pointed to a tall oak tree growing on this open area.

'That's one of the oaks of Mamre, my daughter. Our father Abraham pitched his tent there whenever he stayed near Hebron. In fact, he was there when Yahweh came to destroy Sodom and talked with Abraham face to face.'

'Wasn't he buried in Hebron as well?'

'Oh, yes. In the Cave of Machpelah which is over there.' Naomi pointed with her chin. 'There's a huge rock covering the entrance to the cave still.'

The trial was to be held in the open air and several stools, guarded by a sweating young Levite, had been placed near the oak of Mamre for the judges. People sat or stood wherever they thought they could get the best view of the proceedings and already the branches of the oak were thick with boys and young men determined to be as close as possible to the action. Several times a venerable old man with a grey beard came raging down and ordered everyone out of the tree, but though some descended others swarmed up in their place and eventually the old man sat down on one of the stools, muttering and casting ferocious glances up at the tree behind him.

Ruth took Naomi's hand and pushed and shoved her way through the crowd until she was near the front of the assembly. Not long afterwards several more old men came and sat on the stools. By their costume Ruth recognized that they were priests. Almost at once a band of Levites appeared, leading — and guarding — a well-dressed man, his arm bound up in a sling, and Ruth and Naomi were nearly knocked off their feet as the crowd pressed forward to see the killer.

'Is that the man you gave the drink to?' Naomi asked.

'I think so,' Ruth replied. 'It's hard to tell at this distance when he has his turban on and everything.'

The man in front of Ruth turned round. 'Did you give him a drink?'

Ruth modestly covered her face. 'Yes, my lord. I didn't know who he was, just that he was running on a hot day and was very thirsty.'

Others crowded round and Ruth had to repeat her story several times before the interest of those near her was satisfied. When she was able to look again there were two groups near the judges, the killer and his relatives and the avenger and his family and friends. One of the priests stood up and raised his arms and the crowd fell silent.

'Men of Israel! We are here to do justice between Eldad ben Ahimaaz, whose father was killed four days ago and who is the avenger of his father's blood, and Hagi ben Asriel, who has fled to us for refuge. Let all those who are witnesses in this case come forward to be heard. Let everyone else sit quietly, that justice may be done.'

There was a buzz of voices as everybody sat down on the hard and dusty ground. Soon the only ones standing were the dozen men and women walking up and down with trays of parched corn, baskets of fruit or jars of water to sell to the crowd. Three or four men walked forward, but Ruth guessed that most of the witnesses were already standing at the front on one side or the other.

After a lot of consulting with each other, the judges settled back on their stools and the first witness was called. A Levite with a loud voice stood beside the judges and relayed the gist of what was being said by the witness. The first to speak was the killer himself and after a long speech, during which — Ruth strained her ears trying to hear, the Levite took a deep breath.

'Hagi ben Asriel, of the tribe of Simeon, admits that he killed Ahimaaz ben Jezer, his neighbour. He says that they went together to cut wood and as they worked the head came off his axe and struck his neighbour so that he died. He says that when he saw what had happened he dropped his axe handle and ran here for refuge.'

'It could easily happen,' Ruth whispered to her mother-in-law. 'I have to keep a close eye on the thongs round our axe-head. It's come off once already.'

The next to speak was the avenger of blood. Ruth couldn't hear what he was saying but by the energy of his gesticulations she could tell that he was very angry.

'Eldad ben Ahimaaz says that there has long been a quarrel between Hagi ben Asriel and his father,' the Levite boomed. 'He says that the killing was murder, not an accident and demands the right to avenge his father's blood.'

'I wonder what the quarrel was about?' Ruth mused, half to herself and half to Naomi.

Now several men from the group around the killer stepped forward and spoke long and earnestly to the judges. After a while the Levite raised his voice again.

'Shuni ben Asriel, Eran ben Asriel and Malkiel ben Imnah, relatives of Hagi ben Asriel, declare on oath that their brother is a good man who lived in peace with his neighbours and would not deliberately kill anyone.'

At once two men from the avenger's family placed themselves in front of the judges and shouted angrily. Even without the Levite, Ruth could hear them insisting that there was a quarrel between the murdered man and his killer, for Ahimaaz ben Jezer had accused his wealthy neighbour of ordering his servants to shift the boundary stone between their two fields. As the Levite relayed their words to the congregation, Ruth turned to her mother-in-law.

'What happens if the judges can't decide between them?' she asked.

Naomi put her finger to her lips, but whispered a reply; 'If they really can't decide then they will send the case up to Shiloh, to be decided by the high priest.'

'What if he can't decide?' Ruth wanted to know.

'Then I suppose he would use the Urim and Thummim.'

'The what?'

'The two gems that are placed on the shoulders of the high priest's garment. When the high priest takes a matter to Yahweh for an answer, one stone glows brightly for "Yes" or the other goes dark for "No".'

The next to bear witness were neighbours of the two men. One or two spoke up for Hagi ben Asriel and declared that he was a peaceable man, but most confirmed that there was a quarrel between him and Ahimaaz ben Jezer and several hinted that Ahimaaz' accusation against his neighbour was only too likely to be true. One man even alleged that he too had suffered at the hands of his wealthy neighbour.

'The main problem is,' Naomi told Ruth after the judges had broken off the trial to eat, 'no one saw the murder take place. Only two eye-witnesses, or the confession of the guilty, can convict a murderer.'

When the trial resumed it was already past midday and a number of people left to go home and tend to their animals. Ruth and Naomi were able to press forward so that they were within hearing of the judges. The first witness after the midday meal was the headman of the village. His testimony was brief and to the point.

'My lords, I was aware that there was enmity

between Hagi ben Asriel and Ahimaaz ben Jezer and that Ahimaaz had made an accusation against his neighbour, but I would never have dreamed that it was a killing matter. The elders and I went down to the fields and in our opinion the boundary stone had been moved accidentally when Hagi ben Asriel's ploughman ploughed too close to the line between the fields. We ordered the stone replaced and thought that was the end of the matter. Nevertheless, I think that you should look at this, for this is the murder weapon.'

He stepped forward and placed two objects in the hands of the senior judge. One was a polished wooden staff about two cubits long, the other a crescent of metal about a span long. The judge held the objects without looking at them.

'You say it was murder?' he asked.

'Look, my lord,' the headman replied, pointing at the objects in the judge's hands.

The judge looked down first at the staff. He slid his hand along it to the end and swung it experimentally through the air, then passed it to the priest sitting beside him. Next he looked at the crescent of metal, hefting it in his hand to feel the weight and then turning it over and over, a puzzled expression on his face. Suddenly his eyebrows shot up and he looked up at the headman.

'But this is iron!'

'Yes, my lord.' The headman's voice was sombre.

There was a flurry of movement among the judges as they rose from their stools and crowded round to view the rare and expensive metal. The judge raised his head and looked at the accused man. Ruth's eyes followed his gaze. Hagi ben Asriel looked grey and sick and his mouth was working soundlessly. In that instant she knew that he was a murderer.

'Is this your axe?' The senior judge held out the staff and axe-head.

Hagi ben Asriel pulled himself together with an effort. 'Yes, my lord.'

'Is this the axe that killed your neighbour?'

'Y-yes, my lord.'

'And you claim that you went to the forest to cut wood with this?'

The man tried to speak but could only nod his head.

'There is also this, my lord.' The headman held out his hand and placed something in the hand of the judge, who poked at it with his finger.

'What is this?'

'The leather thongs for binding an axe-head to the handle, my lord. My son found them near the body. As you can see, my lord, they have not worn through. They have been cut.'

The senior judge rose to his feet and Ruth hid her face in her hands, unable to watch the killer's face, terrible in its despair.

'Hagi ben Asriel, give glory to Yahweh. Was this death an accident?'

Ruth wished that she had another pair of hands to press over her ears to shut out the dull, hopeless voice that whispered, 'No, my lord.'

'Out of your own mouth you are condemned. Blood for blood and life for life. You may have this night to put your house in order, but tomorrow, as soon as the sun is risen, you will be taken outside the boundary of this city and delivered into the hands of the avenger of blood.'

There was a shriek and Ruth opened her eyes in time to see the condemned man's wife hurl herself forward, babbling wild pleas for mercy. When the judges avoided her eye and stood up to go she turned to the avenger, offering cattle, land, servants, her daughters and even herself in exchange for her husband's life. The senior judge turned back then, his face solemn and set.

'It may not be, my daughter. There is no blood-price in Israel.'

'No blood-price!'

The woman screamed and tore her garment, ripping it down to her girdle. She was still kneeling there, alternately beating her breast and heaping handfuls of dust on her head, when her husband was escorted away by a group of young Levites armed with staves and swords.

Ruth glanced over at the avenger and was shocked to see his face as grey and bloodless as the murderer's. He stared in horror at the wailing woman in front of him who was now tearing at her face and breasts, her fingernails leaving long, bloody lacerations across her skin. Suddenly he turned and was violently sick.

Ruth felt herself gripped by the elbow and dragged away, but for many steps her head strained back over her shoulder, staring in horrid fascination at the young man and the despairing woman.

'Oh, mother, that was horrible!' Ruth choked when at last they were out of earshot of the distraught woman.

'I know, my daughter. I know.' Naomi's normally cheerful face was sombre and sad.

'What's going to happen now?'

'You heard the judge, my daughter. Tomorrow that man will be taken outside the boundary of the city of refuge and the avenger will kill him.'

'Will they fight?'

Naomi shook her head. 'No, though doubtless the murderer will struggle. He will be bound and there will be those on hand to assist the avenger by holding him down.'

'And he'll just kill him?'

Ruth burst into tears, dabbing at her eyes with her head-cloth. 'It's horrible, horrible. Mother, did you see his face? I don't think he can do it. He might have done it when his blood was hot but not in cold blood.'

'He has to.' Naomi spoke earnestly. 'He has to or he will be shamed forever, a son who would not avenge his father.'

The following day one of the younger men who had relatives living near Hebron returned with news of how the affair had ended. Hagi ben Asriel had appeared very calm that night, calling in his wife and his son and giving them instructions on how he was to be buried and what they were to do after his death. About midnight he dismissed everyone, saying that he was tired and wanted to sleep. Although there were guards at the door and outside the window, there was no one in the room, no one to see him climb up on his bed and tie his girdle to a rafter. In the morning he was dead, his body swaying gently in the breeze that came through the window.

———

The laws mentioned in this chapter:

Cities of Refuge — Numbers 35:6-28.

Urim and Thummim — Exodus 28:30; Deuteronomy 17:8-13.

Gleaning

'But where will I go, mother?' Ruth wailed. 'I can't just walk into somebody's field and start reaping his crop.'

'Of course not, my daughter.' Naomi's voice was patient. 'Just go around the fields until you see a group of reapers working. A poor man will be working in his field by himself or with his wife, but a rich man will have a gang of reapers working for him.'

'Aren't we allowed to glean from poor people?'

'Yes, we have the right to glean anywhere, but a poor man will need all his grain for himself and won't let so much fall whereas a reaper working for someone else won't be as careful.'

Naomi reached out and pushed Ruth's head-cloth back from her forehead.

'Now, off you go, my daughter. You were keen enough yesterday, so I don't know why you've gone shy all of a sudden.'

'I don't know,' Ruth sighed. 'It was different back in Moab. It was like an adventure, sneaking out by night to get what you could. It's different, just walking into someone's field and helping yourself. It's almost like stealing.'

'Don't be silly.' Naomi steered Ruth gently towards the door. 'Look, there's a gang working in that big field down there. Why don't you go and try them?'

Ruth left the hut and walked reluctantly along the path towards the group of twenty or so men and women who were hard at work in the field at the bottom of the hill. Both men and women were squatting down, seizing handfuls of stalks and cutting them off close to the ground with wooden sickles lined with flint teeth. Women and children carried bundles of the cut grain over to a corner of the field where two men drove a pair of yoked oxen around and around to thresh the grain with their hooves. Ruth was surprised to notice that the oxen were not muzzled and wisps of straw hung from their slowly working jaws.

Near the edge of the field there was a rough shelter, a square of palm-leaf matting held up by four poles, beneath which stood several large pottery jars. A tall man stood in its shade, his arms folded, watching the workers. As Ruth left the path and stepped over the field boundary the tall man turned and noticed her. He watched her for a moment and then walked towards her.

'Yahweh be with you.'

'And with you, my lord.'

He looked her up and down, noting her ragged garment and stained head-cloth. 'Come to glean, have you?'

'If you please, my lord.'

The man's eyes narrowed. 'You're that Moabite girl, aren't you?'

'Yes, my lord.'

'Thought so.' The man seemed pleased with his own cleverness. 'Your accent was funny. Ever done this before?'

'No, my lord.'

'Right. It's quite simple, really. You can work anywhere in the field behind the reapers, picking up any grain that has been dropped. Cut a stalk of wheat for yourself and you're off, understand?'

'Yes, my lord.'

'Good. Of course, when work is over for the day you'll have the usual rights to edges and corners. Now, you have your own supplies?'

'Supplies, my lord?'

'Yes, food, drink, the usual. The water in the jars over there is for the reapers. If you're thirsty you go and get your own. Fine, now see that woman over there behind the man with the red head-dress? She's another gleaner. You just follow her and do what she does and you'll be right. Yahweh be with you.'

The tall man turned on his heel and strode off, calling loudly to one of the reapers to stop talking and get on with his work. Ruth walked uncertainly towards the squatting woman, admiring the deft way in which she snatched up stalks of grain from the ground in front of her and added them to the bundle in her arm. The woman shuffled forward continuously, keeping up with the stalwart reaper in front of her.

'Yahweh be with you.'

The woman looked up over her shoulder and to her relief Ruth realized that she had seen her several times at the village well.

'And with you,' the woman replied, smiling. 'Come to glean, have you?'

'Yes, please, sister.'

'I know you.' The woman stood up and massaged the small of her back. 'You're Ruth, Naomi's daughter-in-law. I've seen you at the well a few times. I'm Hoglah, the daughter of Amram the son of Jeruel the son of Judah.'

'How come you're gleaning?' Ruth asked.

Hoglah shrugged; 'The usual. My parents died in the famine and the father of my son was sick all last year with a fever and had to sell himself as a slave to pay our debts.' She sounded remarkably free of bitterness. 'Never mind. Only three more years.'

'What happens then?' Ruth asked, but Hoglah had squatted down and wasn't listening

'Come on, Ruth. Talking won't fill our bellies.'

Without thinking Ruth hitched up her skirts, tucking

the hem into her girdle in the Moabite fashion and leaving her legs free and unencumbered. A chorus of yells and whistles broke out around her and Ruth looked up, startled.

'Shameless!' Hoglah hissed. 'We don't do that here.'

Ruth looked around, blushing. It was true. All the other women, even the reapers, were struggling to work with their skirts down around their ankles. Her first impulse was to pull her garment down, but she was too embarrassed to admit her ignorance of local customs and habits. She would lose less face if everyone thought she had kilted her skirts deliberately.

'We do where I come from,' she said airily, reaching for a couple of stalks.

'Well, I'm just glad you don't come from Egypt,' Hoglah snapped.

'Why?'

'Don't you know? People say that men and women work naked in the fields there.'

The two girls stared at each other for a moment and then burst out giggling.

'Come on.' Hoglah reached for her own skirts. 'I'll keep you company. It's not as if I was unmarried.' She carefully pulled her garment up a few inches, tucked the excess material into her girdle and then squatted down again. 'Now, let's go.'

For the next couple of hours the two girls worked side by side, snatching up the stalks of grain that fell from the hands of the reapers or that were dropped as they passed their bundles of grain to the women who carried it to the threshing floor. When their arms were full Ruth and Hoglah carried their own bundles to the side of the field and stacked them there. Ruth was quite pleased at the way in which her stack grew larger, though she felt uncomfortable when some of the men stopped their work to stare at her legs as she passed.

'Who's that man over there?' Ruth pressed both hands into the small of her back as she pointed with her chin towards the man by the water jars.

'That's Bekr, the son of Shuham,' Hoglah told her. 'He's the lord of the harvest, the man in charge of the reapers. He comes from somewhere the other side of Hebron and he's responsible for the gang working on this field and the one over there, and there's another gang over the other side of the village that he runs as well. Boaz hires him every year.'

'Boaz?' Ruth was startled. 'Does this field belong to Boaz?'

'Yes. Didn't you know?' Hoglah laughed at the look on her friend's face.

'No. Oh, dear, I hope mother won't be too upset.'

'Why? What's wrong?'

'Boaz is related to us somehow and mother is too proud to go and ask him for any help, even though we are poor. I hope she won't be annoyed with me for gleaning in his fields.'

'Well it's too late to worry about that now,' Hoglah's eyes sparkled with mischief, 'because here comes Boaz right now, if I'm not mistaken.'

Ruth turned and looked in the direction Hoglah was gazing and saw the tall, well-dressed figure of her distant relation-by-marriage riding his donkey down the hill towards them.

'Quick!' She grabbed Hoglah's arm. 'Let's get back to work. Maybe he won't notice me.'

Giggling wildly, the two girls ran back to their chosen spot and started gathering up the stalks of grain that had accumulated in their absence. Ruth kept her face resolutely turned away from the village but after a while she couldn't help asking, 'What's he doing?'

Hoglah glanced over her shoulder and whispered

back. 'He's just standing there, talking to Bekr ben Shuham.'

Another few minutes passed and then Ruth asked again. 'Now what's he doing?'

Hoglah straightened up and pretended to rub her back, glancing over her shoulder as she did so.

'Keep your face turned,' she hissed, 'he's looking this way.'

She leaned forward and picked up a few more stalks of wheat, then waved away an imaginary fly as the excuse for snatching another glimpse. Ruth heard her gasp.

'Watch out! He's coming this way!'

Ruth buried her face in her bundle of grain and worked feverishly until two sandalled feet stopped right in front of her and a deep, warm voice said, 'Yahweh be with you, my daughter.'

Blushing furiously, Ruth looked up into a pair of friendly, laughing brown eyes.

'And with you, my lord.'

'You're Ruth, the girl from Moab, aren't you?'

'Yes, my lord.'

The man's lips parted in a wide smile and Ruth found herself admiring his strong, even teeth and his luxuriant, neatly combed beard.

'I thought so. Listen to me, my daughter. Don't go off anywhere else to glean. You're welcome to follow after my reapers until the harvest is over. I see you've found a friend, but if she can't come for some reason and you have any problems, go to my servant girls, they'll look after you.' His eyes dropped to Ruth's bare legs and his lips twitched. 'In any case, I've given the men strict instructions to leave you alone.'

Ruth felt her blush deepen as she stammered her thanks. Boaz nodded and turned to go then stopped and looked back at her.

'Oh, and by the way, any time you're thirsty, just go and help yourself from the water jars over there.'

Ruth heard Hoglah gasp at this unusual privilege and to cover her confusion she bowed down and pressed her forehead to the ground.

'May Yahweh reward you, my lord, but why — I mean, I'm not really related to you. I'm only a foreigner.'

Boaz cleared his throat and when he spoke again his voice sounded strangely hesitant.

'Ah — I — er — I — um — everyone says what a marvellous thing you've done for your mother-in-law by leaving your own people to come and live among strangers so that you can care for her.' His voice became stronger and more confident. 'May Yahweh, the God of Israel, under whose wings you have come to take refuge, richly reward you for your loyalty. A drop of water is the least I can offer.'

Ruth kept her face towards the ground, the rough stalks of cut grain sticking into her forehead. 'May I continue to find favour in your eyes, my lord.'

'He was blushing!' Boaz was barely out of earshot when Hoglah jabbed Ruth with her finger, her face creased by a knowing grin.

'What for?' Ruth protested. 'I didn't say anything wrong, did I?'

'Huh!' Hoglah snorted and then burst into a fit of giggling. 'You certainly knew what you were doing when you tucked your skirt up like that! Maybe I ought to try it.'

'I never!' Ruth felt her face grow hot again. 'We all do that in Moab.'

'Really?' Hoglah eyed her sceptically. 'Well, all I can say is that if ever my husband gets the urge to travel, I'm not going to let him go anywhere near Moab. At least,' she burst out giggling again, 'not in harvest time!'

'What's the joke, you two?'

A man dressed in ragged clothes and carrying a cloth-wrapped bundle stopped near them and smiled in a friendly way.

'Nothing. Nothing.' Ruth was terrified that the man might have overheard Hoglah's inane chatter.

'Women's talk.' Hoglah raised her head haughtily and tried to look mysterious.

'Oh, women's talk.' The man grinned and walked on, leaving a delicious aroma of fresh bread behind him.

'Who was that?' Ruth asked as soon as the man was out of hearing.

'Eliab ben Issachar. He's one of Boaz' servants.' Hoglah sniffed loudly. 'By the smell I'd say that he's come to bring Boaz his dinner and by the way my stomach feels I'd say it's about time too. Come on, let's go and eat in the shade over there.'

———————

The laws mentioned in this chapter:
　　Gleaning — Deuteronomy 24:19-22.
　　Threshing — Deuteronomy 25:4.

A meal of parched barley

Ruth stood up and quickly let her skirt down, vowing silently never to tuck it up again, no matter how inconvenient and cumbersome it was. She followed Hoglah over to the matting shelter where the water jars stood. Although she was thirsty she did not dare help herself until one of the workmen beckoned her over and urged her to, 'Drink, drink.'

When she had drunk her fill she walked over and lowered herself to the ground beside Hoglah, who was resting her back against one of the poles that held up the palm-leaf roof. Hoglah had her lunch out already, a piece of unleavened bread and some greens, and was chewing happily.

'Where's your food?' she asked through a full mouth.

Ruth shrugged. 'I haven't got any.' she confessed.

Hoglah raised her eyebrows. 'Why not?'

'I don't know. I've never done this before. I suppose I just thought I would go back home to eat.'

'No time for that,' Hoglah said. 'Here, share mine.'

She started to tear the piece of bread across but stopped as a tall figure stepped up to Ruth.

'Did you not bring food?'

Ruth snatched at her head-cloth and drew it across her face. 'No, my lord.'

'Come over here. I have plenty. No greens, I'm afraid,' Boaz smiled and nodded at Hoglah, 'but you can dip the bread in the vinegar.'

Ruth hesitated, unsure what a woman in her position ought to do. As a girl in Moab she had heard tales of how wealthy landlords took advantage of helpless women and though she had not expected such treatment from those who followed Yahweh, a girl could not be too careful. She glanced around at Hoglah and was relieved to see her nod approvingly.

'He's your kinsman.' Hoglah mouthed the words.

Ruth heaved herself to her feet, aware, as she did so, of how ungraceful the action looked. 'You are too kind, my lord.'

'Nonsense.' Boaz led the way to the other side of the shelter and the reapers shuffled back to make way for them. Bekr ben Shuham had a small fire blazing in front of him with a bronze pan balanced over it on which he was roasting barley fresh from the threshing floor. He glanced up at Ruth, his face a careful blank, and drew his feet in to make room for her.

'As I was saying, my lord . . . '

Boaz raised his hand. 'Just a moment, Bekr, my friend. Pass that bread, will you?'

Bekr handed Boaz a platter on which stood a large pile of freshly baked unleavened bread. Boaz lifted three of the largest pieces and handed them to Ruth.

'Will this be enough?' He looked at her anxiously. 'I can give you more.'

'This is more than enough, my lord.' Ruth took the bread, letting her head-cloth drop. 'I don't eat very much.'

'Good, good.' Boaz smiled, his teeth flashing. 'The vinegar is in this pot.'

He placed a small jar between them and then turned back to the lord of the harvest. 'You were saying, Bekr?'

'I was saying, my lord, that the harvest is very good this year. Look at these grains. Good and fat.'

He placed a handful of parched grains into Boaz' hand and Boaz poked at them, squeezing them between thumb and finger-nail before tossing the whole handful into his mouth and chewing vigorously.

'Mmmm. I see what you mean. Very good. Here, try some.'

He took the pan from Bekr's hand and tipped its contents into Ruth's lap.

'My lord!' Ruth protested. 'I already . . . ' She gestured towards the uneaten bread she was holding.

'No, no. Really. Try it and tell me what you think.'

Ruth picked up a few grains and placed them in her mouth, aware of Boaz' anxious gaze and Bekr ben Shuham's expressionless one.

'Delicious, my lord.'

Ruth meant it. The grain had a rich, nutty flavour and the foreman had parched it to perfection.

'Splendid.' Boaz smiled again. 'Have some more — that is, if we can persuade the worthy Bekr to parch us some more.'

Bekr ben Shuham said nothing, but the glance he shot at Ruth was not unfriendly. For the rest of the mealtime Boaz behaved as if Ruth were not there, talking busily to Bekr ben Shuham about crop yields, prices in Jebus and Hebron and other details of the harvest. From time to time he reached over and dropped another avalanche of parched grain into Ruth's lap, blandly ignoring her protests that she had more than enough.

Blind with embarrassment Ruth chewed on, dimly aware of the reapers leaving the shelter to continue their work. She didn't even see Hoglah get up and go. Suddenly Boaz stood up and for the first time appeared to notice the heap of grain in her lap. His eyes danced.

'Hmmm. If you can't eat all that you'd better wrap it up and take it back to your mother-in-law. Tell her it's a present from me.'

He smiled broadly at her and then walked away, chatting quietly to Bekr ben Shuham. He appeared to be giving some commands and by the way he kept glancing back at her Ruth feared that they concerned her. It was a relief when he mounted his donkey and with a cheerful, 'Yahweh be with you all', rode back up the hill towards Bethlehem.

Ruth sat there, cramming the remains of the bread into her mouth, wondering what she could do with the mound of parched barley in her lap. Before she reached any decision one of the older women from the gang of reapers came into the shelter and handed her a piece of rough sacking.

'Bring it back tomorrow.' she ordered gruffly when Ruth thanked her, and then stood watching as Ruth emptied the grain onto it and carefully tied the corners together.

'You watch that one.' The woman spoke in a low voice. 'He's after you.'

'What do you mean?' Ruth blushed.

'Don't be a goose.' The woman's friendly eyes belied her harsh voice. 'Anyone can see he fancies you.'

'But he's my kinsman!' Ruth protested.

'Oh, is he? Sorry I spoke!' It was the woman's turn to flush. 'Let's hope he has a kinsman's intentions.' She stepped closer to Ruth and her voice dropped to a whisper. 'All I know is that Bekr ben Shuham has just been round all the men telling them that the boss wants them to show special favour to you. Anything you do is all right, even gleaning among the stacked sheaves. In fact, he hinted that it would be a good thing if they deliberately dropped things in front of you.'

'Never!'

'As true as Yahweh sees me,' the woman nodded. 'So, as one woman to another, watch your step my girl. Of course,' she added, tossing back her head-cloth, 'what you do is your own affair. Master Boaz would be a good catch and you'd not be the first one to make a play for him, but he's kept clear up till now. I don't reckon he's the marrying kind.'

The woman shrugged and made as if to leave, then turned back to Ruth. 'Don't tell anyone I've warned you. I don't want to get into trouble, but we women have got to stick together.'

'No, I won't,' Ruth smiled. 'I'm very grateful, really.'

Hoglah already had half an armful when Ruth squatted down beside her and reached for a stalk of cut grain that one of the reapers had let fall.

'What took you so long?' Hoglah spoke teasingly.

'I guess I'm just a slow eater.'

'Slow eater indeed! I . . . ' Hoglah broke off to stare wide-eyed beyond Ruth. 'There's a bit of luck for you!'

'What?' Ruth asked, turning her head.

'Didn't you see? That man stumbled and dropped his whole armful, right beside you! Look, behind you.'

Ruth craned her head round further to see a huge pile of barley almost at her right hand and a grinning reaper looking down at it. The man winked at her and strolled off, swinging his sickle.

'May Yahweh send me such luck,' Hoglah breathed. 'Go on, girl, get it. He can't pick it up once he's dropped it. That's the rules.'

Ruth gathered up half the grain and then turned and pressed it into Hoglah's arms. 'There's more here than I can carry.' She spoke firmly. 'You need luck just as much as I do.'

'But — but — something like that may never happen again!' Hoglah protested.

'I have a feeling there's going to be a lot of lucky accidents around here,' Ruth said. 'We women have got to stick together.'

The slave

As the afternoon wore on, the pace gradually slackened until Bekr ben Shuham started a traditional harvest song and sickles moved faster in time to its beat as men and women vied with each other to improvise verses while the gang shouted the refrain. They poked fun at each other, at their work and their employer with outrageous similes, ludicrous comparisons and excruciating puns. Some of the verses had Ruth and Hoglah rocking with laughter while at others Ruth blushed for shame.

Just after mid-afternoon the wind changed direction, as it did every day, and dust from the threshing floor blew across the field, making throats dry and voices harsh. Rather than break the rhythm of the work Bekr ben Shuham sent one of the women round with a water pot to give drink to all the workers.

'Sister?' The ragged man Ruth had noticed earlier was standing obsequiously in front of the woman, his cupped hand half raised to his mouth. To Ruth's surprise the woman appeared not to have noticed him and gazed off to one side, the water jar held firmly on her shoulder.

'Sister?' The man repeated, his voice uncertain.

The woman turned her head and looked at the man, then without a word spat straight in his face. Ruth stared in astonishment as the man turned away, wiping his face with his sleeve. From the way he mopped at his eyes she was sure that he was crying.

Ruth looked about her. No one else appeared to have noticed the incident but by the uncomfortable silence she knew that they all had seen and heard what had happened. After a long moment the woman with the water pot stalked away and Ruth bent to her work again. Hoglah caught her eye and grimaced in the direction of the woman's back.

'She's a bitch,' she hissed. 'Hard as flint and not an ounce of pity or forgiveness in her.'

'Who is she?' Ruth whispered back.

'His sister.' Hoglah nodded towards the ragged man. 'What happened was the making of him, but it's made her hard and bitter.'

'Why? What happened?'

Hoglah reached for another cut stalk lying on the ground in front of her and added it to the bundle she held in her arm, then settled back on her haunches.

'You'd never believe that Eliab was once the richest man around here,' she began, gesturing at the ragged man. 'His father, Issachar, was a shrewd, hard-working man who bought cheap and sold dear. I'm not saying he was unfair, mind you, just that he knew when to buy and sell. He never spared himself and worked as hard as any labourer, even though he owned most of the land on that side of the village.'

Hoglah pointed with her chin in the direction of the Arabah.

'His wife died giving birth to Mahlah, Eliab's sister' — Hoglah almost spat the name — 'and Issachar didn't marry again. He brought the two children up by himself and, I'm afraid, rather spoiled them. I suppose he tried to make up to them for the fact that they didn't have a mother. Anything they wanted, they got, and I can remember Eliab galloping through the village in a fancy chariot pulled by a pair of expensive horses, with a couple of men running in front with sticks to clear the way for him.'

Ruth clicked her tongue in astonishment and Hoglah smiled briefly. 'I know. And Israelites aren't even supposed to own horses — they're more for warriors than peaceful farmers. Eliab was always going off to Jebus and coming back roaring drunk or bringing Canaanite friends back here for wild parties. If his father tried to remonstrate with him, he was rude and abusive. Any other father would have had him stoned to death as a rebellious son, but Issachar just smiled and shrugged and paid the bills and told everyone that the lad was only sowing his wild oats.'

Hoglah shuffled forward a pace or two and picked up some more grain before continuing. 'Well, he got a shock when his daughter — her with the water pot — fell in love with one of the lad's disreputable friends, a Canaanite from somewhere the other side of Jebus. Now it was her turn to give the old man no rest, weeping and pleading and threatening to kill herself if she didn't get what she wanted. He was already weakening when the Canaanite lad turned up, sober for once, and swore that he wanted to enter the covenant and worship Yahweh. He even claimed to have circumcised himself and limped around for a couple of days looking pale and brave.'

'Had he?'

'I doubt it,' Hoglah spoke contemptuously. 'Still, it was enough to persuade old Issachar. He held a big wedding with musicians and an Egyptian cook and was very hurt when no one from the village turned up. We couldn't stop him marrying his daughter to whomever he chose, but we weren't going to have any part in it.'

Ruth said nothing and just hoped that her new friend wouldn't stop to think that she was a stranger who had entered the covenant with Yahweh after her marriage to an Israelite.

'I think that boycott made Issachar realize just what he had done.' Hoglah spoke reflectively. 'He seemed to grow old almost overnight. He withdrew into himself and stopped coming to sit among the elders at the gate.

A year later he died and Eliab threw the biggest party of all time to celebrate coming into his inheritance.'

'He never!' Ruth was shocked.

'He did,' Hoglah affirmed. 'As you can imagine, not a single person from the village went — not that we were invited, mind. We hardly saw him for the next two years, but we heard a lot about him, how he was gambling and drinking and chasing women over there in Jebus.'

'Who looked after the farm?' Ruth asked.

'That's just it! The man who had been overseer and steward to old Issacher was so disgusted by what was going on that he went and found another job and although Eliab', Hoglah nodded towards the ragged man, 'stopped partying long enough to come and appoint someone else, the new man cheated him with both hands and hardly went out to the fields at all. After a while he was sacked and someone else, a Canaanite, got the job; but he was, if anything, worse.'

Hoglah tossed her head and her ear-rings shook and sparkled in the sunshine. 'The climax came about three years ago — no, it must have been four years ago, just before the famine ended — when we were all up at Shiloh for Tabernacles. The harvests, as you can imagine, had been disastrous and Eliab's fields, thanks to that Canaanite, produced virtually nothing. He was there, half drunk as usual and making a big noise for himself, when a group of Canaanites appeared and appealed to the judges for justice. It appeared that he was terribly in debt and they were his creditors.'

'No!'

'Oh, yes!' Hoglah's eyes sparkled with unholy glee. 'There was a terrific scandal. The judges enquired into the matter and he couldn't deny it. Right there and then, in front of the tabernacle, they held an auction. All his lands were sold off, his house, his cattle, every thing. Of course none of us wanted the chariot and horses, so the Canaanites got them, at a bargain price. That paid off half his debts and for the rest the Canaanites claimed their right to sell him as a slave.'

'Oh, no!' Ruth's eyes were wide with horror.

'No one wanted to saddle themselves with such a wastrel but when the merchants threatened to take him to Jebus and sell him there Boaz finally stepped in and bought him. Of course that didn't pay off all his debts but Boaz paid a generous price and that shamed some of Eliab's relatives into raising some more money and eventually the merchants went off, grumbling.'

'So Eliab is a slave to Boaz?'

'Worse and worse,' Hoglah grinned. 'When he heard that his brother-in-law had lost everything and was actually a slave, that Canaanite who was so in love with Mahlah suddenly fell out of love and threw her out. She turned up back here literally with nothing except the clothes she had on; her husband had even kept her jewellery — to pay for bringing up her children, he said.'

'How did she live?' Ruth asked.

'She didn't.' Hoglah spoke crisply. 'No one trusted her enough to employ her and by and by she turned up at Boaz' place and begged him to take her as his maid-servant. He's too kind for his own good, that one. He paid off her debts and took her into his household, where she's been ever since.'

Ruth turned her head to hide her blush. 'Does he — I mean — is she — er '

'You mean, is she his concubine?' Hoglah sniggered. 'You should have seen her when he first bought her. All airs and graces, thinking she had it made with the richest bachelor in Bethlehem. "Do you want a drink, my lord?" "Will I rub your back, my lord?" "May I kiss your feet, my lord?" It was sickening. Boaz stood it for two days and then sent her out to work in the fields.'

'Poor girl.' Ruth tried not to show the gladness she felt. 'It must have been a real come-down for her.'

'That it was, and no doubt,' Hoglah chortled. 'For the first time in their pampered lives they had to work, both of them. Got their hands dirty and an ache in their backs and a thrashing if they tried to shirk. Did them the world of good — or at least, it did him the world of good. Eliab's changed, over the years. He's humble, meek, quiet; if anyone can judge such a thing, I'd say that he truly loves Yahweh.'

'And what about Mahlah?'

'Huh!' Hoglah tossed her head. 'She puts all the blame on him. It's all his fault. His fault that the money's all gone. His fault that they are both slaves. His fault that her marriage broke up. She's all hard and bitter and unforgiving, yet when they were well off she was as bad as he was with partying and carrying on. There's some as say' — Hoglah dropped her voice — 'that she only just married that Canaanite in time, if you know what I mean.'

'What does he say?' Ruth felt uncomfortable talking about the other woman and tried to change the subject. 'Does he accept the blame?'

'Yes, he does, fair play to him. He openly acknowledges that he wasted his inheritance. He even accepts the blame for the break-up of her marriage, though truth to tell, what do you expect if you marry a heathen? He says that he's grateful to Yahweh for giving him another chance.'

'Another chance? You mean that he's going to try and save up enough money to buy himself out of slavery?'

'No, silly!' Hoglah stared at Ruth as though she had

lost her wits. 'The Year of Release. You haven't forgotten that, have you?'

'Oh, yes, the Year of Release.' Ruth tried to cover up her ignorance. Fortunately Hoglah was too busy talking to notice anything amiss.

'That's only two years away now and you can trust Boaz to do the right thing. He'll see that Eliab gets some tools and some seed and at the very least the loan of an ox to do the ploughing.'

'But what will he plough? I mean, he hasn't got any land now, has he?'

'Don't forget the Jubilee.' Hoglah spoke with exaggerated patience. 'That comes the year after the Year of Release. Of course he won't get back all the land his father acquired over the years, but he'll have his ancestral portion and that should be more than enough for a man on his own.'

'The Jubilee!' Ruth's eyes sparkled. 'That's when we'll get our land back as well.'

'You, and many another,' Hoglah glowered. 'And there'll be more than one who's been living in luxury these past few years who'll suddenly find themselves with no land and no servants and a whole lot of work to do.'

'No servants?' Ruth queried.

'Of course not!' Hoglah snapped. 'You don't think that my husband will stay as a servant when he gets his own land to work, do you?'

'How did he lose it? or shouldn't I ask that?'

'Ask all you like, my dear. It wasn't he who lost it. It was his father who lost it, same as the young chap we've just been talking about — riotous living and gambling and such like. I doubt he ever drew a sober breath after he inherited the farm. My husband's a good, hard worker, nothing like his father. It's not his fault that he was sick. You'll see. We've got a bit saved up already and he's got his eye on a bull that he saw up at Shiloh one year and that the owner is keeping for him. We'll have to work hard, but one day we'll be rich!'

For the first time that day Hoglah's sad face took on the warmth of a happy smile and Ruth felt a sudden gush of love for Yahweh fill her heart.

'Isn't Yahweh wonderful!' she exclaimed. 'He's given us such a wonderful Law, such a good Law.'

Hoglah looked a little startled. 'Why, I suppose He is,' she admitted.

'Of course He is. We've got nothing like this back in Moab,' Ruth enthused. 'Back there, if you're poor, you stay poor and if you're rich you just get richer and richer and prouder and prouder.'

'Really?' Hoglah's interest was lukewarm at best.

'Really! You people who've lived in Israel all your lives just don't realize how lucky you are. You ought to try worshipping Chemosh and offering your children to Chemosh and watching the priests of Chemosh taking the best of your belongings — and you getting nothing in return. Yahweh is such a kind God! I just wish everybody in the whole world knew about Him!'

'I suppose so,' Hoglah admitted. 'I've never really thought about it.' She bent forward and reached for some more grain.

'And what about her?' Ruth asked, pointing to the woman with the water pot who was making her way back to the field from the well.

'What about her?'

'Well, will she be set free in the Year of Release?'

Hoglah sat back and watched Mahlah for a moment. 'That's a real problem for Boaz,' she admitted.

'But you say that Boaz hasn't — er '

'No, that's the problem. Normally, I suppose, the owner would arrange a marriage for a slave-girl he owned but didn't want, but I doubt there's a man in

Israel who would want to marry Mahlah, no matter how big her marriage portion. I suppose he'll just have to set her free and send her back to live with her brother.' Hoglah grinned sardonically; 'That'll be fun for both of them!'

'Maybe that's what makes her so bitter,' Ruth suggested, 'knowing that in the end she will be dependant on a brother she despises.'

Hoglah shrugged. 'Maybe. Or maybe she's bitter because he will have a chance of getting back what he's lost — his house and land and possessions — but she will never get back what she's lost — her husband and her children.'

'Do you know what I think?' Ruth asked. 'I think that not only is Yahweh's Law good and kind, but those who disobey His Law pay a heavy price. The happiest people I know are those who are obedient to Yahweh in everything.'

The laws mentioned in this chapter:

    Horses — Joshua 11:6.

    Rebellious son — Deuteronomy 21:18-21.

    Year of Release — Exodus 21:2, 7-11; Deuteronomy 15:12-18.

The kinsman-redeemer

As the sun began to sink behind the western hills Bekr ben Shuham clapped his hands and called loudly. At once the reapers stood up, many of them massaging their backs, and carried their last handfuls of barley over to the threshing floor. The threshers unyoked the oxen and led them off up the path to Bethlehem while men and women collected their outer garments and trudged along behind the animals. Bekr ben Shuham came over to the two girls.

'Right, then. You can see where the reapers are up to. The two corners over there and all along the edges as far as there and there,' he pointed, 'are yours by Law. There should be a full moon a little later on tonight, so good luck to you. There's a couple of spare sickles over in the shelter you can use if you're careful with them.'

'May we use the threshing floor?' Hoglah asked.

Bekr ben Shuham shrugged. 'I don't see why not. You look honest enough to leave our grain alone.' He paused and looked quizzically at Ruth. 'And if you aren't, I don't suppose there's a lot I can do about it.'

'Now, what did he mean by that?' Hoglah wondered when the foreman was well out of hearing.

Ruth blushed but said nothing.

'Well, let's get on with it.' Hoglah started towards the shelter. 'We've had a good day, but what we glean has got to last us all year.'

'Look at this!' Ruth exclaimed a moment later. She held out the sickle she had discovered under a sack in the corner of the shelter. Hoglah came over and stared at it. 'It looks like the jawbone of some animal — a donkey or something — only instead of teeth it has flints.'

'And they're held in with gum!' Hoglah poked at the sickle with her finger. 'Ordinary ones are held in with bitumen.'

'It's a bit big.' Ruth swung the sickle experimentally.

'More like a weapon than anything,' Hoglah agreed. 'You could kill somebody with that thing. I'll bet that belongs to Bekr ben Shuham himself. There's two of the ordinary wooden ones here. Put that back and use one of these.'

Armed with their sickles, the two young women started to cut the corners and along the edges of the field. There wasn't a lot of grain left behind, mostly the stalks that had sprung up among the nettles and thistles, but every little bit counted and Ruth and Hoglah worked in opposite directions, harvesting every head that remained.

'I'll need a new skin after this,' Hoglah joked, sucking the back of her hand, when the two met back at their piles of grain.

'Me too,' Ruth sympathized. 'Those thorns are vicious!'

When they had cleared the edges right up to where the reapers had left off they replaced the sickles and then gathered up their stacks of grain and carried them to the threshing floor.

'Whew!' Hoglah whistled as she staggered along under a huge bundle. 'I think this is the best I've ever done as a gleaner. I've never known such a clumsy bunch of reapers. The stuff they dropped! You'd almost think they were doing it on purpose.'

Ruth bit her lip and said nothing. She helped Hoglah roll a large stone over to the edge of the threshing floor, well away from the gleaming piles of Boaz' grain. Each girl took a handful of barley stalks and then they stood opposite each other and took it in turns to beat the heads of the grain against the stone until the last precious kernel had rattled down onto the ground. They tossed the useless stalks to one side and gathered up another handful of barley.

When Hoglah's stack was finished Ruth fashioned a handful of empty stalks into a rough broom and swept the ground around the stone, brushing the grain and chaff into a neat pile. She then scooped up a third of the pile onto Hoglah's head-cloth and spread her own out on the ground underneath. Hoglah stood up and slowly poured the contents of her head-cloth onto Ruth's, allowing the gentle breeze to waft the chaff away while the heavier grain fell in a golden stream.

When her head-cloth was empty Hoglah shook the last bits of chaff and dust off it and spread it out on the ground while Ruth poured the pile from her head-cloth to Hoglah's.

'I wish this wind was a bit stronger,' Hoglah grumbled as they repeated the action for the third time. Ruth smiled. She too was tired and hungry and eager to get home.

It was nearly an hour later before Ruth's grain was threshed and winnowed and bundled up in her head-cloth.

'Look at that!' Hoglah exclaimed. 'I reckon there's two ephahs there. Not bad for a day's gleaning.'

She bent and helped Ruth hoist her bundle onto her head and then Ruth, keeping her head carefully upright, helped Hoglah in the same way. The small parcel of parched grain was already tucked inside her robe and she promised herself that she would give half of it to her new friend in the morning. Just as they were leaving, the ragged man strolled onto the field and coughed noisily to give them warning of his approach.

'It's only me,' he called. 'The lot for first watch

tonight fell on me but I didn't hurry, as I knew you were down here. Yahweh keep you and give you a good night's sleep.'

'And you, my lord,' the two girls chorused.

'Huh!' Eliab laughed. 'No sleep for me, not if I want to keep my job.'

After saying good-night to Hoglah, Ruth looked back from the top of the hill. Tiny flickers of stubble fires showed where other watchmen were keeping guard over the fields, protecting the precious grain from enemies, both animal and human. Ruth walked across to her hut and pushed the rough door open. Naomi jumped up to welcome her.

'My daughter! I've been worried sick. Why didn't you come home for lunch? What kept you so lo . . . ' Her voice died away and her eyes widened as Ruth heaved the bundle off her head. Naomi hurried to help her and the two women lowered it to the ground.

'That must be nearly an ephah!' Naomi's voice was hushed.

'And look at this!' Ruth felt inside her robe and brought out the parched barley. 'I saved it for you. The man who owned the fields gave it to me for lunch.'

'Really? Who was he? Where did you work? A blessing on him for his kindness towards you.'

'Where will I put all this grain?' Ruth asked, smiling to herself. She turned away and began looking in the corner of the hut for a pot. 'Oh, yes, the owner of the fields where I worked: let's see, now. His name was — what was it? — that's right, someone — I don't know whether you know him — called Boaz.'

'Boaz!'

Naomi's voice was a high-pitched squeak of surprise and Ruth turned and spun into her arms, whirling her mother-in-law around in a dance of happiness.

'Do those fields belong to Boaz?' Naomi gasped.

'Yes, mother! Isn't it wonderful? Yahweh guided me straight to a man who is our kinsman. At lunch time, when he saw that I didn't have any food, he even gave me some of his and as much parched barley as I could eat and all this besides.'

Ruth let go of her mother-in-law and the two women looked at each other, smiling and laughing.

'May Yahweh bless him.' Naomi spoke breathlessly. 'He's just like his father after all, showing kindness to us who are living and to Mahlon and Chilion's father, who is dead.' She paused a moment to catch her breath. 'You do realize, don't you, that he is one of our redeemers?'

'You mean, he could buy back our land for us?'

'That's right,' Naomi nodded vigorously. 'We wouldn't have to wait until the Jubilee, then. He also has the ri . . . ' She stopped abruptly.

'What does he also have?'

'Nothing, my daughter. Nothing. I was just thinking.'

'Thinking what?'

'Nothing. Or at least, it may be nothing. I don't want to get your hopes up, my daughter, so don't ask me anything further tonight.'

Obediently, Ruth tried to change the subject. 'He gave me permission to glean in his fields for the rest of the harvest. In fact, he urged me to stay with his workers for the whole of the harvest. He said he had ordered them to leave me alone.'

'May Yahweh's name be praised,' Naomi spoke soberly. 'You stick with his maidservants, my daughter. That way you won't come to any harm. There's many a girl comes back from the threshing floor with a heavier burden than she anticipated.'

'But I thought that sort of thing wouldn't happen among the worshippers of Yahweh?' Ruth objected.

'It shouldn't, my daughter, but human nature is the same all over the world. A man gets a little drunk celebrating a successful harvest and comes across a pretty girl gleaning late, or people are temporarily attracted to each other and find a deserted threshing floor too handy.'

'What happens if they're caught?' Ruth wanted to know.

'It depends.' Naomi found a pot and helped Ruth pour the grain into it while they talked. 'If the girl is free to marry, then the man has to pay her bride-price in full, whatever her father asks, and marry her. Furthermore, he is not allowed to divorce her, ever.'

'But what if it is really a rape? I'd hate to have to marry a man who forced me.'

'Oh, if the girl won't have him — and more importantly, if she can persuade her father to reject him — then he just has to pay the bride-price in full, and that's a minimum of fifty silver shekels. He doesn't get a bride, but equally he isn't saddled with someone who hates him and whom, more than likely, he would hate.'

'What if the woman is already married?'

'Then it depends on where they are caught.' Naomi lifted the full pot and put it back at the side of the room, covering its mouth with a clay saucer, held down with a heavy clod of earth. 'If a couple are caught inside the village or town and she's married to someone else or even just betrothed to someone else, then it's a simple case of adultery. They are both stoned to death.'

'And in the country?'

'If they are found out in the fields or woods Yahweh commands us to assume that the woman is innocent, because she is weaker. The man is put to death but the woman is set free.'

'Really?' Ruth was astonished. 'Why, in Moab — or anywhere else that I know of — it's always the woman who is blamed. She's punished and the man gets off scot-free!'

'Which isn't fair, is it?' Naomi said. 'Rape is like a case of murder, where someone stronger overpowers someone weaker, so why should the woman bear the blame?'

'You make it sound as if Yahweh cared for women,' Ruth commented.

'He does!' Naomi nodded emphatically. 'Did you know that in Israel women can inherit property.'

'What?' Ruth's eyes were shining.

'When we were in Moab — I mean, when our fathers were in Moab before they crossed the Jordan — there was a man called Zelophehad who had five daughters. He died and the daughters came to Moses and the leaders of the congregation and asked that they should be given their father's inheritance, the land he would have been given had he lived.'

'How did they dare!' Ruth breathed.

'I know,' Naomi nodded gravely. 'They say that even Moses looked taken aback. Anyway he went to Yahweh and Yahweh told him that what the daughters had asked for was right and proper, so it became a rule in Israel that women can inherit the family property. Well, you know what happens in Moab and the other nations: all the male relatives — or any male if there were no relatives — would seize the land for themselves and leave the women with nothing.'

Ruth nodded. It didn't happen often, but she knew of two such cases and in both the women involved had ended up as beggars or slaves.

'There was only one condition,' Naomi continued. 'The girls had to marry someone from their own tribe. It makes sense, because otherwise there would be bits of Judah up in Ephraim or across in Reuben and that would cause endless fighting and disputes.'

'So women have rights in Israel!'

'Of course.' Naomi smiled. 'Mind you, we are still

subordinate to men: if a woman makes a vow, her father — or her husband if she's married — can make it void as soon as he hears of it. Knowing the way some women get carried away by their emotions, that's probably no bad thing — and I can think of several men who would be the better off if their wives had been able to nullify their vows!'

Naomi chuckled suddenly. 'When I was a girl there was a woman I knew who was always making extravagant vows to Yahweh and then running to her husband to make it void and save her from her foolishness. Every year, up at Shiloh, she'd come out with something new: she'd promise to pay double tithe or eat only one meal a day or keep Passover twice every year. After a while no one paid any attention to her vows any more because we all knew that her husband would put a stop to her nonsense.

'Well, one year she vowed to have a ritual bath every day, which was quite a sacrifice, as she would have to walk several miles to the nearest running water. I guess that her husband was heartily sick of her silliness, because when she reported to him what she had vowed he just said nothing. When she realized that he wasn't going to nullify her vow she went frantic. She nagged him the whole of that day but he simply smiled and complimented her on her piety. For the rest of her life she had to walk all the way to the brook every morning, take off all her clothes and dip herself right under the water — and believe me, it was freezing cold in winter! She never made another vow in her life.'

Ruth laughed at the woman's discomfiture and then frowned slightly. 'Why does Yahweh command women to take a ritual bath every month? It's not our fault that we become unclean.'

'You and I bathe every day,' Naomi answered, 'but not all have our customs. They say that over in Gilead some of the women only bathe once a month.' She clucked her tongue in disgust. 'Then there are people from other nations who have disgusting habits; Midianite women, for example, who bleach their hair with camel's urine. Yahweh wants His people to be clean and sweet-smelling. In fact, it may sound a bit far-fetched, but I have a theory that those who wash frequently actually have better health than those who don't.'

'Really?' Ruth smiled politely.

'I think that Yahweh wants His people to be healthy, to feel good and to look good. We are not to tattoo ourselves, like the Amalekites, or cut decorative scars in our faces like the Cushites. Yahweh gives us two weeks every month when we can take things easy, for when we are unclean anything we touch becomes unclean. In strict households a woman who is having her monthly course has to rest in the sunshine all day long — which must be a real hardship!'

Both women chuckled and then Ruth asked, 'Do you think that perhaps women aren't really unclean, Yahweh just uses the word to frighten the men?'

Naomi nodded vigorously; 'Definitely. Of course, all that blood and mess isn't very nice, but I often think that it isn't me that is unclean. The blood is washing uncleanness away from me. After all, in the temple the blood of the sacrifices makes things clean, not unclean.'

Ruth smiled broadly. 'So women are really just as clean as men?'

'Take another example,' Naomi continued. 'When a woman gives birth she is considered unclean for six weeks after the birth — twelve weeks if the child was a girl. That gives her a chance to get over the birth before her husband lies with her again — and you know what some men are like. They would expect their wives to go straight from the birth bed to the marriage bed.'

'Why are we unclean twice as long for a girl-child?' Ruth asked. 'It's not our fault if the child isn't a boy.'

'No,' Naomi agreed, 'but not all men see it that way. Some of them get really angry with their wives and treat them shamefully for giving birth to a girl. Well, just think. If a man desires his wife after six weeks, he will desire her twice as much after twelve! I know what Mahlon's father was like after six weeks and I should think that after twelve any anger or resentment would be entirely forgotten, swallowed up by other desires.'

'To think,' Ruth mused, 'Yahweh even cares for women. Oh, mother, isn't Yahweh a wonderful God?'

———

The laws mentioned in this chapter:
Rape — Deuteronomy 22:23-29.
Adultery — Deuteronomy 22:21.
Property — Numbers 27:1-11; 36:6.
Vows — Numbers 30:1-16.
Uncleanness — Leviticus 15:19-30.
Tattoos — Leviticus 19:28.
Childbirth — Leviticus 12:1-5.

Hoglah remarked that Bekr ben Shuham's sickle was more like a weapon than a tool. Many years later Samson was to prove her right, when he killed a thousand Philistines with just such a jawbone. The Israel Museum in Jerusalem has several examples of this fearsome agricultural implement.

The captive

While Ruth ate the meal Naomi had prepared for her, Naomi chewed on some of the parched grain.

'Delicious,' she pronounced, when Ruth had finished eating, 'but a bit hard on my old teeth. Take it with you for your lunch tomorrow.'

'Would you mind if I gave some of it to Hoglah?' Ruth asked.

'Who's Hoglah?'

'She's a girl about my age who was gleaning in Boaz' fields as well. She was very friendly towards me.'

'Hoglah, Hoglah.' Naomi shut her eyes and tried to remember. 'Is she the daughter of Amram?'

'I think so,' Ruth nodded. 'She told me her lineage but I can't remember all of it.'

Naomi grinned. 'She's proud of her lineage, but I'll bet she didn't mention that her mother was half-Moabite.'

'Never!'

'She was.' Naomi settled back comfortably on her haunches, ready to tell the tale. 'Let's see. Hoglah's grandmother, Bath-anath, was one of the women captured by our men when we fought against Moab in the time of King Balak. She was only about 14 or 15 at the time, but very beautiful and there was quite a bit of competition among the men as to who would get her.'

'Brutes!' Ruth muttered.

'Just wait!' Naomi held up her hand. 'Now you must admit, if she had been captured by any other nation she would have been raped by a dozen men as soon as she was caught and probably killed afterwards for pleasure. Our men followed Yahweh's Law, so she was brought back safe and sound. When the booty was divided up, she was given to a man from the tribe of Judah who already had a wife and several children. Of course, most of the captive women were just used as slaves to do all the work, but this man was in love with Bath-anath — or thought he was — and the last thing he had on his mind was putting her to work out in the fields.'

Ruth sniffed disapprovingly but said nothing.

'Yahweh's Law is that a captive woman must be allowed a month in which to mourn for her family and her country, and as a sign of that mourning she must shave her head and put on new clothes. Only after the month has passed can her owner take her to wife.

'Needless to say, the man's wife was furious, and not just because she would have a rival. Because of his position her husband could have had several slaves and quite a few sheep and goats, but he had given them up in exchange for Bath-anath. She gave the girl the oldest, dingiest robe she could find and shaved her head completely. Mind you, Bath-anath wasn't too keen on being wife number two to a man who was twice her age and with the wife's co-operation she kept her head shaved that whole month.

'For a whole month the wife made that man's life a misery. She nagged him, she scolded him, she burned his food. She set the children on him with tears and pleas to "make mummy happy again". She got her mother, her brother and even her mother-in-law on her side and they added their reproaches to hers. Meanwhile, of course, this bald-headed creature, her eyes red with weeping, was wandering around the house, breaking into loud lamentations whenever she saw her prospective husband — a very different creature from the beautiful girl who had first excited his desires.'

'Poor man.' Ruth's eyes sparkled and her voice was not at all sympathetic.

'Poor man indeed,' Naomi chuckled. 'At the end of three weeks he had had enough. He gave in and told his wife that he had changed his mind. She, of course, was delighted and immediately kicked the girl out of the house before he could change his mind again.'

'What happened to the girl?'

Naomi smiled. 'Strictly speaking, he had the right to keep her as a slave or to sell her to someone else. If he had gone to bed with her and then decided that he didn't want her he would have had to set her free without price, but as I say, his wife kicked the girl out immediately, expecting, no doubt, that she would go back to her kith and kin in Moab.'

'Didn't she?' Ruth was surprised.

'No. During that three weeks Bath-anath had kept her eyes open and decided that she preferred Yahweh's Law to that of Chemosh. She liked the way we worshipped and the fact that none of the captives had been offered to Yahweh in the way that Moabite captives are sacrificed to Chemosh. She liked the way we had no king except Yahweh. Most of all she liked the way she was given a month for mourning instead of being raped on the battlefield. She changed her name to Bath-el and went out to where the women were drawing water and begged for shelter. One of the women took her in and while her hair was growing she met the woman's brother who became Hoglah's grandfather.'

'Isn't Yahweh wonderful!'

'He is indeed,' Naomi smiled and stood up. 'But come now, if we don't get you to bed soon I'll never be able to wake you up in the morning.'

At noon the following day Boaz appeared again in the fields, closely followed by Eliab, carrying his lunch. When Ruth and Hoglah went over to the shelter to eat, Boaz hurried towards them, smiling broadly. 'Yahweh be with you both.' He turned to Ruth. 'Have you brought your lunch today?'

'Yes, my lord.' Ruth had her head-cloth across her face so that only her eyes were visible.

'Oh!' Boaz' smile faded. 'I — er — yes, well, good. Er — is Naomi well?'

'Yahweh be praised, my lord.'

Boaz chewed at his moustache. 'Yes — Yahweh be praised. Yes.' He turned and went back to where Bekr ben Shuham was parching barley over his little fire. The two men talked for a while and then Boaz mounted his donkey and went off. As soon as he was out of sight the foreman came over carrying his bronze pan, his face expressionless.

'Master Boaz asked me to give you this, miss.'

Automatically Ruth held out the cloth in which she had carried her food and the foreman poured a panful of parched barley into it. 'Please thank him for me. He's very kind.'

'I think you ought to thank him yourself, miss.'

'Oh, I couldn't,' Ruth protested. 'I'm only a poor girl.'

Bekr ben Shuham looked at her in silence for a moment, then grunted and strolled away. Ruth turned to see Hoglah staring at her.

'You ungrateful little huzzy!' Hoglah's face broke into a grin. 'I wish Master Boaz was sending me gifts of food. I'd know how to be grateful.'

'Yes, but,' Ruth could feel her face growing hot. 'He's just being kind because he's a kinsman.'

'Really?' Hoglah's eyebrows were raised. 'You haven't got any children, have you?'

'No,' Ruth looked puzzled. 'Why?'

'Oh, nothing. Come on, are you going to eat that grain while it is still hot?'

It was dark when Ruth and Hoglah finished

threshing and winnowing their grain, watched by one of the reapers who had the task of guarding the grain that night. Once more both girls had heavy bundles on their heads due to the unaccountable clumsiness of the reapers near them. As they climbed the hill they were startled to hear the sound of donkey hooves behind them and a deep voice calling to them.

'Yahweh be with you, daughters!'

They looked up as Boaz slowed his donkey to a walk beside them.

'Yahweh be with you, my lord.'

Ruth reached up hurriedly and drew as much as she could of her head-cloth across her face.

'Just been checking the next field.' Boaz pointed over his left shoulder. 'Have you had a successful day?'

'Yahweh be praised, my lord,' the two girls chorused.

'And did you enjoy the parched barley?' Boaz enquired, looking directly at Ruth.

'You are too kind, my lord.' Ruth's voice sounded muffled through the folds of cloth across her mouth.

Suddenly Hoglah stopped and gave a short laugh. 'Oh, silly me. I've left something behind. You go on ahead, Ruth. I'll be right behind you.'

'Hoglah!' Ruth screamed after her friend's retreating back.

'You'll be all right with your kinsman,' Hoglah called and disappeared into the darkness.

'Come on,' Boaz urged. 'I'll see you safe to your mother-in-law's house.'

He chirruped to his donkey and set off up the hill and Ruth reluctantly followed, keeping a modest three paces behind him. He spoke mainly about the crops, asking how it compared with those in Moab and enquiring whether the reapers were treating her well. When they reached the hut Naomi came outside immediately to investigate the sound of a male voice but when she recognized Boaz she bowed low and urged him to come in and eat and rest.

'Yahweh be praised, mother. I have eaten and am satisfied.'

'At least let your handmaid wash your feet, and give you water to drink.'

'My thanks to you, mother, I will come another time.' He flicked the stalk of barley in his hand against his donkey's rump and the animal trotted away into the darkness, leaving only the sound of his voice wishing them Yahweh's blessing for the night.

'It wasn't my fault, mother.' Ruth spoke defensively as soon as he was gone. 'He came upon us in the dark and then Hoglah said that she had forgotten something and ran back down to the threshing floor.'

Naomi gave her a curious look. 'Be at peace, my daughter. He is our kinsman.'

The next night Boaz appeared behind them again, though this time Ruth kept a firm grip on Hoglah's arm, despite her protests that she needed to speak to someone in the next field. Naomi was prompt to meet them, but again Boaz declined her offers of food or drink. Ruth and Naomi stood side by side and watched him accompany Hoglah through the village gate.

'Does he not find favour in your eyes, my daughter?' Naomi asked Ruth.

'He's very handsome — and kind, mother.' Ruth led the way into the hut and sank gratefully down on the ground. 'It's just that he's so rich and we're so poor. I feel shy whenever he speaks to me. I don't know what to say or do. He must think me so stupid.' She leaned forward and idly drew a pattern in the dust with her finger. 'Anyway, doesn't Yahweh's Law say that a Moabite may not enter the assembly of Israel, even in the tenth generation?'

'Who told you that?' Naomi looked startled.

'Oh, it's just something I overheard some of the workmen saying today.'

Naomi considered for a long minute of silence. 'What you say is true, my daughter, but always remember: you are no longer a Moabite. You have entered into the covenant with Yahweh and therefore you are one of Yahweh's chosen people.'

'But surely any other Moabite could accept Yahweh's covenant?'

'Yes, that is true, my daughter.'

———

The laws mentioned in this chapter:
Captive women — Deuteronomy 21:10-14.
Moabites — Deuteronomy 23:3.

Passover

'I'm very grateful for the grain,' Ruth groaned, 'But am I looking forward to the end of the harvest!'

'Don't forget the wheat harvest,' Hoglah laughed. 'That comes straight after the barley harvest.'

'Oh, no!' Ruth rubbed her back and groaned again. 'I'm sure I've never worked this hard in my life.'

'Don't you know the old rhyme?' Boaz was sitting sideways on his donkey, the better to encourage the two women as they climbed the hill with their loads of grain on their heads. He threw back his head and began to chant in a nasal voice.

> 'Two months to pick olives
> Two months to plant grain
> Two months to plant vegetables
> A month to hoe up flax
> A month to harvest barley
> A month to reap and thresh the wheat
> Two months to tend our vines
> A month to gather summer fruit.'

'Beautiful,' Ruth complimented Boaz. 'You have a good voice.'

Boaz shrugged off the praise. 'We plant the grain at the start of winter, to take advantage of the rain. Five months later we reap it, just before the full heat of summer.'

'First the work, then the fun,' Hoglah commented.

'What fun?' Ruth asked.

'Passover,' Boaz answered for her. 'It should come at the start of the barley harvest but this year it is late. I imagine that next year we will have an extra Nisan so that the months come in their proper places.'

'Oh, yes!' Ruth exclaimed. 'And this year, for the first time ever, I'll be able to celebrate it at Shiloh. It must be wonderful to see everyone there — all the crowds, the merry-making, the worship. Mother used to tell me all about it when we celebrated on our own in Moab.'

Boaz said nothing, but when they reached the hut and Naomi came out to greet them as usual, he climbed down from his donkey and spoke to her. 'Your son's wife tells me that you are going to Shiloh for Passover.'

'If Yahweh blesses us, my lord. It would be good to go and give thanks for our safe return to the land of my fathers.'

'Hmmm,' Boaz stroked his beard and fidgeted. 'I wonder — I mean — the roads, you know, could be dangerous. Well, I mean, not dangerous as such, but . . .' He seemed strangely nervous. He took a deep breath and spoke hurriedly, his words falling over each other. 'What I wanted to say was, would you do me the honour of allowing my servants and I to escort you to the feast?'

'We could not dream of putting you to so much trouble,' Naomi protested. 'Two poor women? No one would bother with us.'

'No trouble!' Boaz urged. 'No trouble at all. I'm going anyway. You could just come with us.'

'But we could just go with everyone else in the village.'

'Ah, yes, the village.' For a moment Boaz seemed lost for words. 'But they might go too fast for you — I mean — too slow — I mean . . . ' His voice died away and he shrugged his shoulders and spread his hands.

Naomi waited for a moment and when he remained silent she bowed deeply. 'Well, if you insist, my lord. We would be most grateful.'

Boaz' face lit up in a smile. 'Excellent. We'll go

together.' He flicked his donkey and trotted away into the darkness.

'What about me?' Hoglah's plaintive voice asked as soon as he was beyond hearing. 'Suppose someone robs me between here and the gate?' All three women burst out laughing.

'I'll go with you,' Ruth offered.

'Don't be silly!' Hoglah laughed. 'I can look after myself that far.'

'We're lucky to have a kinsman like that,' Naomi sighed.

'I never heard of a kinsman so eager to do his duty!' Hoglah nudged Ruth with her elbow.

'If only he will make up his mind.' Naomi turned to go back into the hut.

'What are you two talking about?' Ruth demanded, looking from one to the other.

'Nothing,' Naomi said as she went through the doorway. 'Nothing, my daughter.'

Ruth turned to Hoglah, but her friend just shook her head. 'Ask her,' she said, pointing with her chin towards the hut. 'I just wish I was as lucky as you.'

The next evening Boaz stopped at the hut again, to say that he had decided to travel by donkey cart and there would be room for them to travel with him. The following night he invited Naomi to share in his Passover lamb.

'I've got my eye on a big fat one,' he boasted. 'There'll be plenty for all of us.'

'When do we leave, my lord?' Naomi asked as Ruth hovered silently beside her, one hand holding her head-cloth across her face, the other stretched up to balance the load on her head.

Boaz glanced up at the moon. 'Another three or four days, mother. With Yahweh's blessing we'll have all the barley in by then.'

The next couple of days were a whirl of frantic activity. Ruth gleaned by day but in the evening she helped her mother-in-law mend and wash their garments, pounding them on the flat stones beside the well until all the dirt was shaken and washed out of them. They spread them over the bushes behind the hut and left them there all night and all the following day. In the evening they gathered them in again, sun-warm and sweet smelling.

'Tell me about Passover,' Ruth demanded as they sat outside the hut in the first light of day, patching the rents in Ruth's work robe while she wore her only other garment.

Naomi talked happily, retelling the story of the Exodus and the slaying of Egypt's firstborn, of the forty years of wandering when the unfaithful people were not allowed to celebrate the Passover and the joy when they finally held the feast on the very borders of the land of promise.

'They were not allowed to circumcise during those forty years either. They had rejected Yahweh, so Yahweh rejected them and would not admit them to His covenant. Only after they crossed the Jordan, at Gilgal, were they allowed to circumcise and enter the covenant, like Abraham.' She chuckled softly. 'My grandfather told me that although he was still sore and had to walk around very gingerly, that was the best Passover he ever celebrated. To know that their reproach was taken away and that once more they were at peace with Yahweh was the happiest feeling in the world.'

For Ruth, the journey to Shiloh was one of the happiest experiences of her life. Boaz, Eliab and another servant sat at the front of the donkey cart while Ruth and Naomi sat at the back. The Passover lamb, its legs securely bound, bleated noisily between them on the pile of food and bedding, while they and the men exchanged happy banter with one another or with the people who crowded on to the road around them.

'I just can't believe I'm really here!' Ruth whispered to Naomi as they passed a group of Simeonites led by a man with a large drum, who were singing and dancing along the road to Shiloh. Greatly daring, she joined in the shrill ululations of the Simeonite women as they cheered on a young man who whirled and stamped in the middle of the road, his feet raising little puffs of white dust as he danced, and the women laughed and shouted greetings and questions as they passed.

'Where are you from, sister?'

'Why do you ride while we walk, O princess?'

'Yahweh bless you, sister. May you have a thousand sons.'

Another group sang as they strode along, men and women clapping as they raised their voices in praise to Yahweh, the Creator, the one who had led them out of Egypt. A reed flute soared above their voices as the musician, his cheeks puffed out and his eyes closed tight, improvised wild flights of grace notes while the women's bracelets clashed and jingled to the rhythm of their song.

'Everyone is so happy!' Ruth exclaimed.

'Why not?' Boaz turned his head to smile back at her. 'A good harvest makes for good spirits.'

'You'd have an even better harvest if you muzzled your oxen,' Ruth shot back.

'What oxen?' Boaz looked puzzled across his shoulder.

'The ones treading out the corn on the threshing floor.'

'But we can't.' Boaz frowned and Ruth wondered if she had spoken too boldly. 'Yahweh forbids us to muzzle the oxen that tread the grain.'

'Don't tell me Yahweh even cares for animals?' Ruth was intrigued.

'Oh, yes.' Boaz handed the reins to Eliab and swung his legs round so that he could face her. 'Yahweh cares for all His creatures. Why should an ox work all day on an empty stomach when it could eat the hay on which it is treading?'

'In Moab we always muzzle the ox, in case it eats any of our grain,' Ruth told him.

Boaz shrugged; 'With Yahweh's blessing we have enough grain for ourselves. We don't miss the little bit the ox might eat. Take another example: if we come across an ox or ass fallen beneath its load or into a ditch, we must stop to help the creature even if its owner is our enemy. The need of the animal must override our feelings for its owner.'

'Maybe that's just Yahweh trying to get you to be friends with the owner,' Ruth argued. 'What about the wild animals or the birds? Surely Yahweh is too great to notice them.'

He shrugged again; 'I don't know, but the Law says that if we find a bird's nest with eggs or young in it, we may take the eggs or the chicks but we may not touch the mother. We leave her to raise another family and to comfort her mate.'

'Is that why you have so many more birds in Israel than we do in Moab?' Ruth wondered.

'Pesky things!' Eliab growled without turning his head. 'They eat all the grain. I spend the whole time between planting and reaping scaring birds out of the fields.'

'Some do,' Boaz nodded his head. 'And then we get our revenge by eating them: birds like pigeons and doves. Others don't. You know, the other Sabbath I was walking down by the fields and watching the birds diving into the crop. My hand was just itching for a stone to throw at them when I noticed that they were eating some sort of grub or worm. I looked a bit closer and — do you know what? Those caterpillars were eating the crop — not the birds.'

'So the birds were helping you!' Ruth exclaimed.

'Looked like it,' Boaz grinned. 'Mind you, on a week day I would never have noticed. Just hurled a stone and gone on. I guess that's the blessing of the Sabbath: it gives you a chance to watch and learn things like that.'

'Like my husband's mother seeing the deer and its fawn.'

Boaz hadn't heard the story, so Ruth told it to him, forgetting to cover her face in her enthusiasm for the tale and the secret garden.

'I think Yahweh wants us to respect all life.' Boaz nodded his head. 'One of His rules is that you mustn't boil a kid in its mother's milk.'

'But that makes the meat especially tender,' Ruth protested.

'Perhaps,' Boaz smiled. 'It also shows great cruelty and insensitivity towards the feelings of the mother. That milk should be bringing life to the kid, not cooking it. We should respect life, not treat it with callous disregard.'

'If Yahweh cares so much for the animals, how come we sacrifice animals to Him?' Ruth asked.

'I've often wondered that,' Boaz admitted. 'Mind you, when Yahweh first created the world He gave Adam and Eve a diet of fruit and vegetables and nothing else. Only after the Flood, when all the vegetables were destroyed, did Yahweh allow us to eat animals. Probably a diet of just vegetables and fruit would be better for us.'

'Poor people like us hardly ever eat meat,' Ruth observed.

'Well, you'll get some tomorrow' — Boaz nodded towards the bleating lamb — 'I'll tell you something else. When we kill an animal, we do it quickly and painlessly. The priests, who are the only ones allowed to kill animals, have special knives that are so sharp the animal doesn't feel a thing.'

'How can it not feel a cut?' Ruth protested.

'Some years ago I took a vow to be a Nazirite. That meant that I had to be totally clean for Yahweh for a period of time — three months in my case. I had to be extra careful about avoiding anything dead or unclean, and to make sure I stayed careful, Nazirites are not allowed any wine or strong drink; we couldn't even eat raisins, just in case they have fermented. At the end of the three months I went up to Shiloh and got one of the priests to shave off my hair, which is the way you end a Nazirite vow. He used a bronze razor and trimmed my head right down to the skin. The thing was, that afterwards I looked in a basin of muddy water to see what I looked like and I noticed that my head and face were just covered with cuts — yet I hadn't felt a thing while he was doing it.'

'So how do you kill an animal?' Ruth asked.

'We lay it on its back, then the priest makes a single cut across its throat with a very sharp knife. The blood gushes out and in a very short time the animal is dead. Blood is the life, so we always let all the blood pour out on to the earth.'

'You compare that with what the Cushites do,' Eliab spoke up. 'In the days when I lived in Jebus I met an Egyptian who told me that the Cushites often eat a cow alive, cutting pieces off it and eating the meat raw until there is nothing but bones left.'

'That's barbaric!' Ruth's eyes were wide with horror.

'I know,' Eliab shrugged. 'Yahweh's ways are so much better and kinder. Praise to His Holy Name.'

'Amen!' Boaz and the women joined in the glad affirmation.

Late the following day the cart wound round a hillside and came in sight of the little village of Shiloh, perched on its low hill. Below it, on a long, flat spur, stood the tabernacle, the white linen walls of its court-yard flapping idly in the breeze, the smoke of the evening sacrifice trailing up into the cloudless air.

The valley floor around the hill was filled with a huge crowd of people, the white head-cloths of the women standing out amid the multi-coloured robes of the men, and children ran and whooped in every direction. Hawkers strode through the crowd crying their wares and jugglers and contortionists gathered knots of laughing people around them. Rough booths of cloth or matting dotted the plain, each one marked by a thin, blue column of smoke from cooking fires, while the shafts of up-tilted carts rose into the air, the yokes forming unlikely crosses against the reddening sky.

'Where will we find room to stay?' Ruth gazed over the scene with dismay.

'Don't worry,' Boaz chuckled. 'We from Bethlehem always camp over there by those trees. I imagine that there'll be enough room for us.'

Twenty minutes later, after tedious jolting over the rocky ground and through the teeming crowd, familiar faces surrounded them and friendly hands assisted them down from the cart and helped them unload, set up their shelter and unyoke the donkeys.

'Just in time!' a dozen voices chorused. 'They'll be starting to slay the Passover soon.'

As the sun dipped below the horizon the harsh note of a shofar, the ram's horn trumpet, sounded from the hill and the Bethlehem group joined the throng making for the tabernacle, half a dozen lambs bleating loudly as they were dragged along at the end of thin strings. As they passed one campfire a dog barked loudly and a frightened lamb broke its lead, racing off in frantic flight pursued by yelling men and laughing boys until it was surrounded and brought back in triumph.

The crush was most dense at the door of the tabernacle where sweating Levites yelled themselves hoarse trying to produce order from chaos, as each family or village group pushed forward, trying to fight their way to the front to have their animal sacrificed. Naomi plucked at Ruth's sleeve and drew her back, out of the crush.

'Yahweh be praised, we women stay outside,' she mouthed through the tumult.

The women stood back a little while the men and animals slowly pushed their way through the doorway and into the courtyard. Ruth stood on tiptoe and caught glimpses of the scene within, where priests in white robes splashed with blood hurried from group to group, gleaming knives clutched in their blood-stained hands. A pile of bloody lamb-skins grew steadily higher at one side of the courtyard while the flames on the great bronze altar roared and flared as priests reached up to throw the fat and intestines of the slaughtered animals onto the metal grill.

'What's inside the tent?' Ruth shouted into her mother-in-law's ear.

Naomi pulled her back to where the noise was less intense. 'Inside there the tent is divided into two rooms, one behind the other. The first contains a table on which bread is placed every week, one loaf for each of our tribes, an altar on which incense is burned and an oil lamp that is divided at the top into seven small lamps. The second room contains the Ark of Yahweh's Covenant and the Seat of Mercy, a golden throne on which Yahweh sits.'

'What does Yahweh look like?' Ruth drew her head-cloth over her face as a gesture of respect, for she meant no harm by her question.

'No one knows, my daughter. They say that when the high priest goes in there he only sees a glow of bright light, brighter than the sun, in which there is neither form nor shape.'

'So the high priest actually sees Yahweh!' Ruth's eyes shone in the firelight from the altar. 'In Moab our priests only ever see an image of Chemosh — unless Chemosh appears to them in a dream or vision.'

'He actually sees Yahweh's presence, with his natural eyes,' Naomi affirmed.

'Has anyone else ever seen Yahweh?'

Naomi shook her head. 'Alas, my daughter. At first we all might have had that privilege, for Yahweh appointed us all as priests to the nations, but before the tabernacle could be built our fathers sinned and worshipped a golden calf. Yahweh chose instead the tribe of Levi and more particularly those of the house of Aaron, but they too proved unworthy, for two of Aaron's sons became drunk and went into the presence of Yahweh with common fire. After that only Aaron and the high priests after him were allowed into the second room, and even then, only once a year.'

'Oh, I wish I could see Yahweh!' Ruth sighed.

'So do I, my daughter. I would fall at His feet and tell Him how much I love Him and thank Him for all His goodness towards me.'

'And I,' Ruth spoke solemnly, 'I would praise Him without stopping for His wonderful Law, for only a God who is wise and kind and good above all other gods could have given a Law so — so — Oh, mother! Isn't Yahweh a wonderful God!'

And both women raised their hands, tears streaming down their faces, and joined in the psalm of praise — praise which rose above the shouting of the crowds and the bleating of the lambs in a paean to Yahweh, the God above all gods, the Creator, the Redeemer, the Law-giver, who chose Abraham and Isaac and gave them His Covenant, who led our fathers out of Egypt and gave them this land, who cares for widows and orphans, who welcomes prostitutes and pagans beneath His covering wings.

'Praise Yahweh!
Praise His Name!
You servants of Yahweh,
Who minister in His house
In the courts of Yahweh's house.

For Yahweh has chosen Jacob,
Israel is His treasured possession.
Yahweh is greater than all gods,
Yahweh does whatever pleases Him,
He sends lightning and rain and wind from
    His storehouse.

Yahweh struck down the firstborn of Egypt,
He sent signs and wonders against Pharaoh,
He struck down nations and kings.
Yahweh gave their land as an inheritance,
An inheritance to His people Israel.

Your name, O Yahweh, is forever!
Your fame, O Yahweh, is for generations!
For Yahweh vindicates His people,
Yahweh has compassion on those who serve
    Him.

> O house of Israel! Praise Yahweh!
> O house of Aaron! Praise Yehweh!
> O house of Levi! Praise Yahweh!
> Everyone! Praise Yahweh!
> Praise Yahweh!'

The laws mentioned in this chapter:

Muzzled ox — Deuteronomy 25:4.
Bird eggs — Deuteronomy 22:6.
Fallen donkey — Deuteronomy 22:4.
Nazirite vow — Numbers 6:1-21.
Kid in mother's milk — Deuteronomy 14:21.
Blood is life — Leviticus 17:13, 14.
Day of Atonement — Leviticus 16:1-10.

Boaz' song is a translation of the Gezer calendar, a limestone fragment with this rhyme scratched on it, which was found near Gezer. The olive harvest began in mid-September.

The psalm is an adaptation of Psalm 135.

Ancient Israel counted the months by the phases of the moon, which meant that every year they were eighteen or nineteen days short of the full 365. Six times in every nineteen years they added in an extra first month — Nisan — thus having a year with thirteen months. As the feasts were tied to the lunar cycle while the harvests went by the annual seasons, the barley harvest did not always fit in neatly with the Passover celebration.

The plot

'That is the end of the harvest, mother.'

Naomi's eyes met Ruth's across the jar into which they were pouring the grain so carefully gleaned. Neither woman said anything as they looked around the room at the twenty-seven earthenware jars that held the grain Ruth had brought home. With care there was enough grain in each jar to last the two of them for ten or twelve days, but that would not see them through the year, even without the need to barter some grain for oil and wine and other necessaries.

'What are we going to do?'

Naomi carefully shook out Ruth's head scarf, making sure that every grain went into the jar, then she took Ruth's hand and drew her across the room to the doorway. 'Shall I tell you what you must do, my daughter?'

Ruth said nothing, just raised her head and looked full in Naomi's face.

'I've been thinking. It's time you were settled down in a home of your own, with a good man who will care for you.'

Ruth caught her breath and stared at her mother-in-law. She knew that older women arranged marriages for the girls of a household when there was no man to undertake the duty, but whom did Naomi have in mind? Had one of the workmen, the reapers, spoken for her?

She thought of Boaz, tall, handsome and well-to-do. There was a time when she had dreamed that he was in love with her. He seemed more than kind towards her, but though he was still kind and appeared to enjoy her company nothing further had happened. Passover marked the high point of their relationship, but now the harvest was ended and she would probably not see him again until next year. Girls of her social standing didn't mix with important men like Boaz every day of the week.

'You tell me that you have been working with Boaz' servant girls. Now Boaz is quite closely related to us — and that means that he has certain responsibilities to us.' Naomi paused and looked lovingly at her daughter-in-law. 'You see, I knew Boaz when he was just a boy. I can remember watching him play in the street outside our house. Boaz was always kind — but he's been more than kind to you.'

Ruth blushed and looked down at the floor. 'I know, mother. I did think that he — I don't know, I even hoped . . . '

Naomi reached out and patted her hand. 'I understand. But remember: I know Boaz. Have you ever wondered why a man of his age and with his wealth is still not married? There's more than one girl has made sheep's eyes at him through the years, but his trouble is that he can't make decisions — he never could — not until he is forced to, not about women, anyway.'

Ruth shrugged; 'But I can't force him.'

Naomi raised her eyebrows and looked steadily at her. 'Can't you?'

There was something in her tone that made Ruth jerk her head up and look steadily at her mother-in-law. 'What do you mean?' she breathed.

Naomi leaned closer and lowered her voice. 'Are you willing to take a risk — for Boaz?'

'Oh, yes,' Ruth whispered. 'Anything.'

Naomi heaved herself to her feet and walked over to the back of the single room. She stood on tiptoe and reached up into the thatch where it met the top of the mud wall. When she came back she was carrying a couple of small pots. She sat down again and held one of them out to Ruth.

'What is it?'

'Open it, you silly girl.'

Ruth twisted the piece of wood that was jammed into the neck of the clay vessel and pulled it out. She peered down into the pot, holding it round to the light, a puzzled look in her eyes. Suddenly her face cleared. 'Kohl!' she squealed. 'Mother! Where did you get this?'

Naomi's normally impassive face beamed. 'And look at this.' She held out a second pot and Ruth's eyes widened as she recognized the pale yellow gleam of Egyptian alabaster. She took the pot and carefully loosened the stone stopper.

'Mother! Myrrh! Where did you get it?'

'It's nearly empty, I'm afraid. Mahlon's father gave it to me for my wedding present and I've kept it all these years.'

'Are you sure that you . . . '

Naomi snorted. 'Don't be silly. I'm too old for that sort of thing. Who would look at me now?'

'What do you want me to do?'

'Well, first of all go and bathe. After that we'll see.'

Ruth jumped up and kissed her mother-in-law then seized a large clay jar and hurried down to the well by the village gate. In a very short time she was back, balancing the full jar on her head. She disappeared round the back of the hut where, sheltered by the bushes, she washed herself thoroughly. When she came back into the hut her hair was wringing wet and drops of water stood out on her brown skin and soaked her ragged dress.

Naomi led her out of the hut and sat her down on the log beside the door, then began to tease the tangles out of her hair with a wooden comb. The two women chatted while Naomi plaited Ruth's hair, her fingers flying as she twisted the braids, rubbing in a little butter to make the hair shiny and attractive.

When the job was finished Naomi carefully outlined Ruth's eyes with the kohl and then the two women went back inside the hut and Naomi opened the wooden chest and pulled out a clean head scarf and a white gown. Ruth gasped as the fine linen gleamed in the dim light.

'Mother! What — where — how did you get that?'

Naomi smiled secretively. 'I still have one or two friends, you know.'

'But this!'

'Nothing's too good for my girl — but you be careful with it.'

'I will! I will!'

Ruth reached out and fingered the cloth. Thin, almost transparent, the Egyptian linen felt as light and as soft as thistledown. The neck and sleeves were embroidered with fine-spun woollen thread dyed in brilliant reds and blues. It was a garment fit for a queen. Ruth stripped off her dusty, sweat-stained clothes and Naomi helped her into the long linen robe and tied the head cloth around her hair. She stood back to admire the effect and then raised her hands to her ears.

'Now these.'

'Mother!'

Ruth leaned her head to one side and then the other as Naomi gently inserted the heavy rings in her ears. She had never seen Naomi without those ear-rings; although they were only gilded bronze, they were the family reserve, only to be sold in dire emergency. Even more, they were a memorial of Naomi's husband and doubly precious. Tears filled Ruth's eyes at the thought that Naomi should entrust her with something so valuable.

'Shall I put on the perfume?' Ruth gestured towards the alabaster phial.

Naomi shook her head. 'No. As I said, there's not much left and I don't know how much of its virtue it has kept after so many years. This is what you must do, my daughter.'

Naomi took Ruth's hand and led her over to the side of their hut furthest from the road. She pulled Ruth down to sit on the little wooden stool, then squatted beside her and lowered her voice to little more than a whisper.

'Go to the threshing floor as soon as it is dark for Boaz and his men will be there with all the reapers to celebrate and to guard their grain. Mark where Boaz is and watch him carefully, but don't let him see you. When the festivities are over he'll look for a place to sleep near his grain. Follow him. As soon as you are sure he's asleep put some of the perfume on, then go up to him, uncover his feet and lie down beside him.'

Ruth gasped. She could hardly believe that her mother-in-law, the guardian of her virtue, should be advising her to behave in this wanton manner. 'But mother! What will I do when he wakes and finds me there?'

Naomi pursed her mouth and looked prim. 'You just do whatever he tells you, my girl, like any good wife.'

The two women burst out laughing and then Naomi bustled about preparing their evening meal while Ruth sat, self-conscious in the fine linen dress through which her slim body gleamed like copper. When the meal was ready Ruth spread her old clothes over herself to protect the borrowed garment while she ate.

Darkness came rapidly, but Ruth waited until the

sky was spangled with stars before she stood up, embraced her mother-in-law, and set out from the house. It wasn't difficult to pick her way by starlight along the familiar track. Pin points of red light flickered on every side, as happy harvesters prepared to celebrate and guard their grain through the night, but Ruth found her way unerringly to the fields where she had laboured for the last six weeks.

At the edge of the field Ruth paused, taking in the scene. A bonfire blazed in one corner of the field by the threshing floor. Even at this distance she could hear the loud, raucous laughter of the twenty or so men and women who sat around the fire. Bekr ben Shuham was singing a plaintive, wailing song about a girl with eyes like a horse's and teeth like a flock of sheep.

Ruth crept closer and almost screamed when something pressed against her leg. She could feel it cold and wet through the thin linen dress. She looked down and made out the wagging tail of one of the dogs. Had a stranger approached, the dogs would have barked and attacked, but they recognized Ruth and welcomed her with doggy grins. Ruth rubbed a couple of them behind their ears and then stole onward.

There was a tree about twenty cubits from the fire, its lower branches long ago lopped for fodder or firewood, but its trunk was wide enough for Ruth to stand behind, hidden in the darkness. She leaned against its smooth bark and strained to recognize Boaz. At first she didn't see him, for he was sitting with his back to her. Only when he spoke, his deep voice compelling attention from the merry-makers around him, did she recognize his tall silhouette and from then on her eyes never left him.

A woman stumbled to her feet, snatched off her headscarf and knotted it about her hips as she began to dance, hips swaying, arms outstretched and fingers snapping in time to the foreman's song. The others laughed and joined in the song, clapping to its rhythm. A man leaped up and danced with her, jerking and posturing as he circled round her while the other men shouted encouragement and the women ululated. Abruptly the woman stopped, looked about her self-consciously and sat down but another girl immediately took her place, her plaits flying as she gyrated until suddenly they came undone and a cascade of long black hair flowed down over her face and the men cheered and laughed.

One after another they all took their turn to dance out their joy until finally Bekr ben Shuham's wife, a withered, scrawny woman, stood up and moved stiffly to the music, her arthritic hips creaking, her arms fluttering gracefully in gestures that had been old fashioned even when she was a girl. None of the men joined her and for a long moment she danced alone, a pathetic figure whose dancing days were past. The singing faltered as some of the younger girls turned their faces away to hide their sniggers, and then Boaz stood up.

A workman held out his head scarf and Boaz took it, tied it around his hips and moved forward into the firelight. The woman looked up, her face unhappy in its loneliness, and recognized her husband's lord. She froze and cringed away, dreading his rebuke and then, as Boaz raised his arms and snapped his fingers, realized his intent and a smile flooded over her face, washing out the wrinkles and bringing with it a triumphant flash of former beauty. Her step quickened and the song rose higher and Ruth's heart ached with the splendour of her loved one's gesture.

The trap

Several hours passed. Mosquitoes whined and hummed about her, driving her nearly crazy as she fanned or snatched at them, careful lest incautious movement or sudden sound betray her hidden presence. The wine-skins gradually emptied, but she noted with approval that Boaz did not drink to excess. One or two of the younger reapers, mere boys, were already curled up by the fire, fast asleep, when Boaz finally rose and stumbled away into the darkness.

By sheer chance he passed not an arm's length from where she stood behind the tree and Ruth held her breath for fear of discovery, but his fire-dazzled eyes did not see her nor his tired brain detect her presence. She turned and followed him with her eyes, noting the light blur of his woollen cloak as he lay down and drew it up to cover him from head to toe.

For another hour Ruth stood silently behind the tree, the stars majestic above her. Only when the other men were all asleep — apart from the watchman, who was too intent on the fire to notice anything beyond its circle of red light — did she push herself away from the tree and drift silently towards the place where Boaz lay, her linen dress shining in the starlight.

Half-way there she remembered the jar of myrrh. She halted and eased the stopper out of the mouth, then inserted a finger and scooped out a little of the cold, creamy paste. The sweet smell was so strong it nearly took her breath away and she glanced uneasily back at the fire lest the scent betray her. She rubbed the paste into her neck and arms and then self-consciously smeared a little between her breasts before replacing the stopper and tucking the jar back in her girdle.

She stooped silently over Boaz, her eyes straining to tell which was his head and which his feet. Gently she untucked the cloak from around his legs, drawing it half-way up his shins, exposing his feet to the cold night air. She noticed that he still had on his sandals and her womanly instincts urged her to take them off for him but she dared not disturb him too much.

She lay down beside him, near enough to sense the warmth of his body, but not quite touching him. The ground was cold and hard and the stubble pricked her uncomfortably through the thin linen of her garment. As the hours passed and the night grew colder, almost unconsciously she pressed herself closer to the sleeping man until he rolled over and to her surprise she found her head resting on his outflung arm.

Several times Boaz shifted uneasily in his sleep, his feet pawing for the cloak that she had so carefully tucked up around him. If she hadn't been so cold herself, Ruth could have laughed. Instead she pressed herself against him, moulding the contours of her slender body to his, soothing him back to sleep with soft, half-spoken sounds. Suddenly she knew that he was awake, his consciousness flaring like a light between them even as he thrust back the cloak from over his head and held her arm with a grip so fierce that it left bruises.

'Who . . . who's there?'

He sat up and peered through the darkness at his willing captive.

'It's me,' she stammered, the abruptness of his wakening serving to make her voice sound sufficiently frightened. 'It's me, your servant Ruth.'

The man let go of her as if she burned him. The whites of his eyes stared at her, large and gleaming in the starlight. Ruth took a deep breath and leaned towards him. 'Spread your cloak over me — again,' she whispered.

Boaz groaned and fell back, his mind racing. However hard he racked his brain he could not remember seeing Ruth at the harvest supper. How did she come to be here, by his side? How long had she been there? If there was one thing of which he was certain, it was that Ruth was different. She was no trollop, like some he could call to mind; she was a nice girl, respectable, modest; yet here she was lying beside him!

Boaz could think of only one explanation. That new wine must be more potent than he had imagined. Ruth must have come late and he must have made a fool of himself with her — in public, too! Boaz groaned again. What had she said? Spread your cloak . . . ? What if she were pregnant? What a scandal that would be!

Ruth reached out and ran her fingers through his beard. 'You are my kinsman.' Her voice was soft and throaty. 'My redeemer.'

She lay down slowly, nestling her head on his shoulder in such a way that the expensive perfume could not fail to reach his nostrils, and wriggled under the welcome warmth of his heavy cloak. Boaz groaned again, but his arms instinctively reached out and encircled her, drawing her close to his body.

She was so small and light, he marvelled. He'd never held a woman before. And the smell! Sweet, alluring, rich with the promise of unknown delights. What was it she had said? He stilled his churning mind and tried to remember. Kinsman? Redeemer? Of course! A wave of relief washed over him. There need not be any scandal at all. No one to point the finger at him for marrying beneath him or marrying a widow. She was a relative — by marriage it was true — and . . .

Boaz grunted and almost sat up as another thought

struck him. Why, it was his *duty* to marry her! Ruth was a widow without a son — and the nearest male relative was enjoined by the Law to marry such a woman and raise up seed for the dead husband, to carry on his line and inherit his land.

'Bless you, my girl,' he said, his voice a deep rumble in her ear. 'I was afraid that you were in love with one of the young chaps working for me. I hardly dared to think that you would even look at an old fellow like — well, I mean, I am a bit older than you, not much, mind, just a bit.'

He broke off as Ruth nuzzled into his neck and whispered something that distracted his thoughts entirely. It was some time before he remembered about his duty.

'Listen. Don't you worry about anything. I'll see that you get your rights. I should have remembered about being your kinsman long ago. I'll see about it first thing in the morning. It's just that I've been so busy . . . '

He fell silent as a disturbing thought floated across his mind. 'There's just one thing, though. There is someone else — a man called Machir — who is a closer relative than I. Hmmm. I wonder whether he . . . . Mind you, if he is willing you'll be all right, but . . . '

His voice died away as Ruth squeezed him hard, her arms around his neck. 'Stay a while longer,' He begged. 'If he won't act as your kinsman, I swear by Yahweh that I will.'

He turned to her with rising passion and Ruth wondered how to emerge from the situation with her honour intact. There was a momentary distraction — as Boaz kicked at the cloak, trying to get it to cover his feet, and Ruth, smothering a giggle, sat up and peered down at the cloak.

'Are your feet cold?' she asked in a whisper. 'You

poor man, they must have come uncovered somehow. Shall I rub them for you?'

She slipped out from his embrace and knelt down by his feet, taking them in her lap and warming them in the way her mother had shown her. Her father had loved it, Mahlon had loved it — and men were all the same, her mother said. When she was sure that Boaz was asleep again she curled up, his feet pressed into the pit of her stomach, and drew the cloak over her.

But Boaz was not asleep. For a while he luxuriated in the soothing massage of his feet and allowed himself to relax, but when Ruth lay down again and went to sleep he stayed awake, going over what he must do on the morrow. Under no circumstances was he going to allow that old skinflint to get his Ruth. The trouble was that she was so beautiful. He smiled grimly to himself as he thought of Machir's wife. Even in her youth her only attraction had been the size of her dowry, and he could well imagine her reaction to a rival. Yet for Ruth, his kinsman might even be willing to brave his wife's wrath.

Suddenly he remembered Elimelech's land. It wasn't much, but it was good land, fertile, near to water. What if he proposed a split in duties; he took Ruth and his kinsman took the land? If he knew anything about old Machir, faced with a choice he would prefer the land to any number of beautiful girls. But what if, faced with such a choice, Machir should go contrary to the habits of a lifetime and choose the girl — choose Ruth? It was unthinkable. Anyway, wasn't there some way by which he could have both land and girl?

The first birds were only just stirring in the nearby trees when Boaz arose and gently wakened Ruth. She sat up, yawning and rubbing her eyes, her garment unconsciously but provocatively slipped off one shoulder.

'Come here,' Boaz whispered, and she stumbled to

her feet and came towards him. 'Hold out your head cloth.'

Ruth pulled the square of white material off her head and held it out while Boaz poured a full measure of barley into it — and then another and another. At six measures he had to stop as Ruth's arms were beginning to sag under the weight and the cloth would hold no more. She squatted and knotted the scarf tightly around the gift. Boaz bent down and helped her lift the bundle and balance it on her head.

Boaz watched as her erect figure disappeared down the road to Bethlehem, hips swaying, the fine linen swishing around her ankles. One of the men sleeping beside the ashes of the fire sat up, cleared his throat noisily and spat. Boaz was beside him in an instant.

'If anyone ever hears that there was a woman on the threshing floor through the night,' he hissed, 'you're fired, Jabez, and I'll see to it that you never work round here again!'

The man stared up at him, the pale light of dawn illuminating his scraggly beard and pinched features. 'A woman, my lord? I never saw any woman.'

In the dim light it was impossible to be sure whether that slight flicker of an eyelid was a wink or not.

As soon as she was out of sight, Ruth broke into a near run, despite the load she was carrying. She glanced down at the now crumpled and dirty linen, so transparent that she might as well have been naked. That was all very well for a fine Egyptian lady in one of those fairy-tale palaces, but it would not do for a peasant girl like her to be caught in such a dress, painted and plaited like a harlot. Her face burned at the thought of meeting one of the other women coming to the well to draw water or carry food out to her man at one of the other threshing floors.

To her relief she met no one and Naomi was waiting

by the open door, her face tired but expectant. 'How did it go, my daughter?'

Naomi's eyes widened as she took in the size of the bundle Ruth was carrying and all questioning was suspended as she helped her lower it to the floor. 'He gave this to you?'

Ruth fell into her mother-in-law's arms and kissed her. 'Yes. Six measures! Mother! That's as much as I could have gleaned in two or three days! And he promised to act as our kinsman.'

'He did? What did he say? How did he react when he found you beside him? When did he wake up?'

The questions came pouring out faster than Ruth, her eyes bright with tiredness, could answer them, but gradually the story was told and every detail, every word, analysed for hidden significance. At last the two women fell silent and Ruth sat still, exhausted by her emotions.

'Now what shall I do, mother?'

'Nothing.' Naomi was definite. 'You just sit still and do nothing. I know Boaz, remember? Now that he has given his word he will not rest until he has done everything that he promised. He'll be here before nightfall to tell you in person — good news or bad.'

'But what about that other kinsman — that Machir? What if he insists on being my redeemer? I couldn't bear to marry someone like that!'

Naomi took Ruth's head and pressed it against her chest. 'Trust me, my daughter. Boaz will think of some way to outwit him. Don't you worry about him at all. Now come on, let's get you out of those things and into something less splendid but more suited to the wife of a man like Boaz.'

———

The laws mentioned in this chapter:

Levirite marriage — Deuteronomy 25:5, 6.

The redeemer

As soon as the sun rose and the other men were awake, Boaz excused himself and hurried down the road towards Bethlehem. He went to his house, had a wash and changed his clothes, ate a meagre breakfast and then, composing his features to appear calm and relaxed, set out for the gate. He strolled through the market place, calling leisurely greetings to everyone he met.

There were three old men already sitting on the plaster bench in the gateway, enjoying the warmth of the morning sun, when he arrived. Boaz greeted them and sat down beside the oldest.

'Yahweh be with you,' he said.

'And with you,' they answered.

'Are you in health?'

'Yahweh be praised, we are in health.'

'Yahweh be praised. And your families also?'

'Yahweh be praised, our families are in health also.'

'Yahweh be praised.'

Boaz' eyes were dancing with mischief or merriment, and now they lit up as he saw Machir, the older relative, coming up the slope towards the gate, yawning mightily after a night among the sheaves. 'Ho, Machir!'

Machir swallowed a yawn and sauntered across to Boaz.

'Yahweh be with you, Machir.'

'And with you, my brother.'

'Are you in health?'

'Yahweh be praised, I am in health. Are you in health?'

'Yahweh be praised. Is your family in health?'

'Yahweh be praised.'

Machir's eyes flickered up the street towards his yet unvisited house where his family and breakfast awaited him. 'Is your family in health?'

'Yahweh be praised.' Boaz patted the seat beside him and Machir reluctantly sat down.

'Are your crops good?'

'Yahweh be praised, my crops are good. And your crops? How are they?'

'Yahweh be praised. My crops are . . . ,' Boaz broke off the reply to call to another old man who was hobbling slowly down the street towards them. The old man blinked with surprise at being greeted so enthusiastically but accelerated his pace as the ritual words of benediction and praise passed between them, until he sank with a sigh onto the bench opposite Boaz. Machir half rose and instantly Boaz turned back to him. 'My brother! Is your grain safe?'

'Yahweh be praised, my grain is safe. Is your grain safe?'

'Yahweh be praised.' Boaz grinned to himself, remembering the events of the night before, and then he spotted another ancient emerging from the front door of his house. He called to him and soon a fifth old man was sitting contentedly in the gateway, exchanging greetings with Boaz and the other elders. Machir slipped his feet into his sandals and reached for his staff.

'My brother! Are your reapers satisfied with their wages?'

Machir sat back reluctantly and allowed his sandals to slip to the ground again. 'Yahweh be praised, they are satisfied. And your reapers?'

'Yahweh be praised.' Boaz eyed him, a tiny grin twitching his beard. 'Have you eaten well, my brother?'

'Yahweh be praised, I have eaten well.'

The palpable lie, with the air heavy with the smell

of the cooking fires, widened Boaz' grin. He looked up in time to spot another of the village elders and called him over to join the five already sitting at ease in the gateway.

By the time the ninth old man was sitting on the bench Machir was extremely restive, but every time he showed signs of getting up Boaz turned to him and continued what seemed an inexhaustible litany of greetings and polite enquiries. It was obvious to all, including Machir, that he was being detained for some particular reason and several younger men, scenting something unusual in the air, drifted up and stood motionless nearby, watching the group in the gateway expectantly.

When the tenth village elder arrived everyone sensed that the serious talk was about to begin. Ten was a quorum, the *minyan*, the minimum number necessary for worship or for business. Almost casually Boaz turned back to Machir. 'I hear that Naomi wants to sell that piece of ground that her husband owned over by the sheep fold.'

Everyone turned to stare at Boaz. This was news indeed. Elimelech had hung on to that piece of ground as long as possible. Only when it was sold and the money all but used up had he undertaken the long trip to Moab to avoid his creditors and the shame of being sold as a slave.

'You are older than I,' Boaz added. 'You have the right to redeem the land.'

Of course, the land would come back to Naomi in the year of Jubilee, but that was still a few years in the future. What she was offering now, however, was the right of redemption. Land could not be sold to strangers in perpetuity but between family members was a different matter. Whoever bought from her the right of redemption might then, if he wished, open negotiations with the present owner and add the land to his own inheritance, more or less in perpetuity — particularly as the only possible claimant, Naomi herself, was a childless old woman.

'Now, in the presence of our brothers, tell me whether you will exercise your right or not.'

Everyone's eyes turned to Machir. No one would actually call him a miser — not to his face, anyway — but there was no denying the fact that whatever fell into his hands tended to stick there.

There was a moment of silence. A hungry, greedy look passed over Machir's face and his eyes closed slightly as he weighed up the cost of redemption against the profit he could expect and the enlarged inheritance he could pass on to his son. 'I will redeem it.'

Boaz uncrossed his legs and put both feet flat on the floor. His duty was done. The man who had the right of redemption had been told of Naomi's wish and the village elders could be relied upon, now that they had been officially informed, to make sure that Naomi got a fair price and that Machir didn't delay matters unduly in order to force her to accept a lower price.

Boaz reached for his staff and stood up. 'Yahweh's blessing on all of you.'

The elders turned to Machir and congratulated him on his purchase. Boaz started to walk away and then stopped, as if a thought had just occurred to him. He turned back to Machir. 'By the way, you do realize that it is a joint sale?'

'Joint?'

'Yes.'

'What do you mean, joint?'

'Well, Ruth, you know, the Moabite girl that Mahlon married; if Naomi has an heir I suppose Ruth is the heir. Whoever acts as kinsman to redeem the land will also have to act as kinsman to Ruth and give her a son.'

Boaz turned away again but his heart was singing at the look of dismay on Machir's face. Everyone knew what a shrew his wife was. It would take a braver man than Machir, Boaz reckoned, to go and tell her that he was bringing a beautiful, younger woman to share his home.

There was another factor as well. Although any son Ruth might bear would be counted as Mahlon's child, by tradition he would also share in Machir's property, thereby diminishing the inheritance passed on to Machir's other children. Boaz wondered which motive was uppermost in Machir's mind — fear of his wife or love for his son.

Machir cleared his throat. 'My brother!'

Boaz stopped and looked over his shoulder.

'I — er — I cannot redeem the land.'

Boaz said nothing, just raised his eyebrows.

'I cannot mar my son's inheritance.'

Boaz swung round towards Machir, his face a fine mixture of scorn and rage. 'You refuse to do your duty as a kinsman?' he exclaimed.

Machir hung his head miserably.

'You refuse to do your duty to our dead brother!'

The elders shifted uneasily on their seats while the younger men nudged each other and pressed forward so as not to miss a single word. By explicit command in the sacred Law of Moses, a man who refused to do his duty to his brother in this matter was forever shamed. The rejected widow had the right to come and publicly spit in his face and remove his sandals, leaving him barefoot and disgraced.

'Just wait until Naomi hears about this! Just wait until Ruth hears about this! She'll . . . '

As Boaz raged he nearly laughed aloud for joy. It would do no harm to blacken his relative's face just a little, just enough so that he would never dare to make trouble over that piece of land in the future. At the same time he was aware that he had to be careful not to provoke Machir too much. He didn't want to lose what he had won.

Once or twice, as the elders added their reproaches to Boaz' words, Boaz feared that he might have gone too far. Several times Machir seemed about to speak but each time he subsided again. Suddenly he bent down and pulled off his own sandal.

'I know, I know, but I just can't.' Almost pleadingly he held out his sandal to Boaz. 'Here, take this. Why don't you be the kinsman? You're not married. I give you all my rights in this matter.'

Boaz slowly reached out and took the sandal, his face thoughtful as if the idea had not occurred to him until that minute. He looked round at the assembled elders and the other men pressing about them. 'Very well. I accept. You are all witnesses that I have this day bought the right of redemption to the land that was Elimelech's. I will act the part of kinsman towards the widow of Mahlon, Elimelech's son.'

'We are witnesses,' the crowd chorused.

Boaz handed the sandal back to Machir. 'You agree?'

'I agree.'

'Yahweh be praised!'

Though he was bursting to rush to Naomi's little hut and give Ruth the news, he forced himself to sit down again and pass the time of day with the elders and the other men in the gate, accepting their congratulations and blessings with an indifferent shrug.

'May Yahweh make this girl like Rachel and Leah!'

'May your marriage make you famous in Bethlehem!'

Machir sat silent, glowering at the happy group around Boaz. Already he was regretting the impulse that had led him to pass up both girl and land. At last he stood and turned towards Boaz.

'May your family be like that of Perez, whom Tamar bore to Judah.' He turned and walked away in a dead silence. Tamar, the Canaanite girl who bore twins to her father-in-law and Perez, the child who made a breech in the birthright of his brother — it was an insult and all eyes turned to Boaz to see his reaction.

Boaz had heard the words and with one part of his mind understood the affront, but most of his mind was in a daze of happiness and all he could think of, all he cared about, was getting away as quickly as possible and going to Naomi to ask for the formal permission he was sure would be granted.

'May Yahweh bless you too, my brother,' Boaz called after his relative's back.

He stood up, his feet slipping easily into his sandals. He beamed round at the crowd in the gate.

'Yahweh be with you all. I have some — ah — urgent business, some — well — in fact — some urgent business. I have to see a man — er — a woman — about a piece of land.'

———

The laws mentioned in this chapter:

Levirite marriage — Deuteronomy 25:7-10.

The last word

The story of Ruth is too well known to need re-telling. Rather, this little book is an attempt to show how the Law of Moses worked in the daily life of Palestine in comparison with the harsh rules of other lands. Those who wish to go into the matter further may find it instructive to read the provisions of the Code of Hammurabi, which some believe was contemporary with Moses.

David, the psalmist, and Paul, the evangelist, both declare that 'God's Law is perfect' and God Himself, speaking through the prophet Ezekiel, claimed, 'I gave them my decrees and made known to them my laws, for the man who obeys them will live by them. I also gave them my Sabbaths as a sign between us, so they would know that I, Yahweh, made them holy.' (See Ezekiel 20:11, 12, NIV.)

These Laws were the basic rules of an egalitarian and tribal society where there was no centralized authority, no police, no prisons. The punishments imposed, if sometimes harsh, were none-the-less fair and swift. They were surrounded by safeguards that protected the innocent and the weak, for whom, indeed, God showed special regard.

These Laws came to an end when the nation of Israel was destroyed in AD70. As civil regulations they play no part in the Christian — or any other — religion, though they provide a model of justice and humanity that many modern nations would do well to copy.

'Yahweh' is a commonly accepted vocalization of the sacred Tetra-grammaton, YHWH. Although in later years the Jews deliberately refrained from using the divine name, its frequent occurrence in the Psalms and in everyday speech recorded in books such as Ruth indicates that the children of Israel referred to God by the name He had proclaimed, as unselfconsciously as the people of other nations referred to Baal, Chemosh or Re-Harakhte — or Christians speak of Jesus.

'My lord' is a translation of 'adonai' and is used much as we might use 'sir', as a polite way to address a stranger or someone of superior status.

Apart from Ruth, Naomi and Boaz, all the other characters are inventions, their actions and motives based upon my acquaintance with people in the Middle and Far East, plus a vivid imagination. If some of the characters seem a little too earthy I refer my readers to any newspaper for evidence that this is what ordinary people are like — and to the Song of Songs for confirmation that the people of God were not immune to human passions or averse to expressing their feelings in earthy, not to say explicit, language.

Index to the laws